# PRAISE FOR *THE WRONG WOMAN*

'A twisty small-town PI mystery with a protagonist I didn't want to let go'  **IAN RANKIN**

'J.P. Pomare has given us another juicy small-town read . . . Expect plenty of twists and turns in this thriller'  **WOMAN'S DAY**

'Fresh and complex . . . delivers on every front'  **ARTSHUB**

'The definitive J.P. Pomare whodunnit . . . rich with red herrings and clues alike, drip-fed to the reader, enticing them to unravel the mystery. Pomare is, in every definition, a masterful page-turner . . .'  **GOOD READING**

'Captures you from page one and then barrels along with all the hallmarks of a J.P. Pomare thriller – a twisty plot, unforgettable characters and, more importantly, heart'  **CHRISTIAN WHITE**

'Pacy, tense, atmospheric, masterfully plotted and suspenseful, with more than one satisfying twist. You'll be gripped right up till the final page'  **ROSE CARLYLE**

'An expertly plotted mystery with echoes of Lee Child. I raced through it and missed it once I finished'  **ALLIE REYNOLDS**

## PRAISE FOR *THE LAST GUESTS*

'A twisty thriller . . . Possibly not one to read in your rented holiday cottage. I'll certainly be checking the light fittings at my next beach holiday rental'
**THE AGE**

'*The Last Guests* is a brilliantly executed siege set-piece that keeps readers guessing until the final few pages'
**GREG FLEMING, stuff.co.nz**

'This is a rip-snorting read that burbles along on fine prose, from a novelist who while still early in his career has already stamped his mark as a masterful storyteller. An excellent read from a must-read author'
**GOOD READING**

'A twisty thriller with an ending I didn't see coming'
**MEGAN GOLDIN**

'Carefully constructed, chilling and compelling, Pomare's latest creation will keep you guessing right up to the last page'
**ROSE CARLYLE**

'Chilling . . . Should keep readers up at night. Pomare knows how to keep the pages turning'
**PUBLISHERS WEEKLY**

'An emerging master of the taut and fast-flowing psychological thriller'
**ARTSHUB**

# PRAISE FOR *TELL ME LIES*

'A deliciously tight and twisty tale that is guaranteed to keep you turning the pages into the wee hours. If you enjoy your psychological thrillers at a breakneck pace . . . then add this to your wish list'

**GOOD READING**

'Some startling surprises towards the end and a dark, thoughtful conclusion will keep you frantically turning the pages'

**CANBERRA WEEKLY**

'A thrilling story about a celebrated psychologist who gets too close to a patient' **WHO MAGAZINE**

'J.P. Pomare spins another intriguing tale in his latest thriller'

**READER'S DIGEST**

'The acclaimed author of *Call Me Evie* and *In the Clearing* returns with this twisty psychological thriller' **WEST AUSTRALIAN**

'A twisty tale full of suspense and mystery' **NEW IDEA**

'*Tell Me Lies* is a fast-paced mystery thriller'

**SYDNEY MORNING HERALD**

'A whodunit with a limited number of possibilities that encourages the reader to guess between a handful of possibilities' **HERALD SUN**

## PRAISE FOR *IN THE CLEARING*

'*In the Clearing* is written with a technical aplomb that proves *Call Me Evie* was no fluke'  **THE AUSTRALIAN**

'Will keep you on the edge of your seat and wide awake until you've raced to the end. A true psychological thriller that is totally believable and which will stay with you long after you've finished'

**HERALD SUN**

'Both [Pomare's] books are testament to the fact that he could be one of the most exciting literary thriller authors to come out of the country'  **SATURDAY PAPER**

'There are lots of premium crime-fiction offerings this summer, but this bloodcurdling exploration of the asphyxiating grip of a cult on its followers deserves to be at the top of your pile'  **NEW DAILY**

'A very fine thriller from a very fine author' **NEW ZEALAND LISTENER**

'If J.P. Pomare's *Call Me Evie* was a slow-burner of a psychological thriller, his follow-up, *In the Clearing*, is a pared-back firecracker'

**BOOKS+PUBLISHING**

## PRAISE FOR *CALL ME EVIE*

'Almost nothing will turn out as it initially appears in this devastating novel of psychological suspense'

**PUBLISHERS WEEKLY (starred review)**

'Read this one with the lights on, and keep Pomare on your radar'

**KIRKUS REVIEWS**

'A whip smart debut from our newest thriller star'

**NEW ZEALAND HERALD**

'I felt pure dread reading this book. Enjoyable, exquisite dread'

**SARAH BAILEY**

'It's a tight, compulsive, beautifully written thriller with echoes of Gillian Flynn, with characters that keep you guessing and a plot that keeps you turning the page'       **CHRISTIAN WHITE**

'A striking and suspenseful read'       **SYDNEY MORNING HERALD**

'Will have you guessing and second-guessing until the very end'

**HERALD SUN**

'A one-sitting kind of book, ideal for readers who enjoy fast-paced thrillers that keep them guessing'       **BOOKS+PUBLISHING**

'Pick this one up when you have plenty of time as you're unlikely to put it down after a few pages'       **DAILY TELEGRAPH**

# HOME
# BEFORE
# NIGHT

**ALSO BY J.P. POMARE**

*Call Me Evie*
*In the Clearing*
*Tell Me Lies*
*The Last Guests*
*The Wrong Woman*

# J. P. POMARE

# HOME BEFORE NIGHT

Hachette

# ⊞ hachette

First published by Amazon Audible Originals in 2022
Published in Australia and New Zealand in 2023
by Hachette Australia
(an imprint of Hachette Australia Pty Limited)
Gadigal Country, Level 17, 207 Kent Street, Sydney, NSW 2000
www.hachette.com.au

Hachette Australia acknowledges and pays our respects to the past, present and future Traditional Owners and Custodians of Country throughout Australia and recognises the continuation of cultural, spiritual and educational practices of Aboriginal and Torres Strait Islander peoples. Our head office is located on the lands of the Gadigal people of the Eora Nation.

A catalogue record for this book is available from the National Library of Australia

ISBN: 978 0 7336 4954 7 (paperback)

Cover design by Debra Billson
Cover photographs courtesy of Shutterstock
Author photograph by Leah Jing McIntosh
Typeset in Adobe Garamond Pro by Bookhouse, Sydney
Printed and bound in Great Britain by Clays Ltd, Elcograf S.p.A.

The paper this book is printed on is certified against the Forest Stewardship Council® Standards. McPherson's Printing Group holds FSC® chain of custody certification SA-COC-005379. FSC® promotes environmentally responsible, socially beneficial and economically viable management of the world's forests.

In memory of Jerry Kalajian

The bond between a mother and her child is the only real and purest bond in the world, the only true love we can ever find in our lifetime.

– Ama H. Vanniarachchy

# PROLOGUE

IT WAS A hot day, if a little overcast. Lying on a towel on the sand, she could feel herself growing sleepy as the sun crept across the sky. The beach was almost entirely theirs. Three teenaged boys threw a frisbee at the other end toward the point and up on the cliffs behind her, a couple of surfers were assessing the swell, leaning against the bonnet of their station wagon. Parked beside it was a tiny blue hatchback. She looked back to the sea, there was a calm patch close in. It's a steep beach that drops away sharply when you get near the water where the waves break hard against the sand. That calm dark patch looked so cool and inviting. She could just slip in for a moment, rinse the sun's heat from her skin then come back to her boys on the beach. She was so tired those days – no-one told her how long the sleepless period would last – a dip would freshen her up.

'I might cool off in the water,' she said.

He looked over at her, took a long sip of his beer. She saw the ocean reflected in the aviator sunglasses he'd picked out at the service station. Her two-week-old son was in the Moses basket between them. She never thought it would be possible to have a baby. She had given up on the idea altogether, until it happened – suddenly, miraculously she was pregnant. Then late in the night, through the heat inside and the exhaustion, the endless, back-arching, excruciating pain, her son arrived.

'Bit rough out there,' he said, nodding at the sea. He finished his can and tossed it by the others on the sand.

'I'll go where it's still, in the shallows over there.'

She pulled herself up, lifted her son from the basket and held him to her, kissing his forehead, before laying him back down. Lastly she adjusted the muslin cloth covering the basket to keep the sun off him. 'Won't be long.' She glanced back once at the cliffs. It didn't bother her that he'd been drinking, but she knew she couldn't indulge too much, she couldn't do anything at the moment. It was hot and he had grabbed a couple of beers on the way here. She had a few sips of his can, letting the beer sit in her mouth. It all felt so normal, so peaceful.

Maybe, she thought, just maybe they could have a normal happy life, maybe they could be a boring family, shift to the suburbs, take up hobbies. Anything was possible. That moment could be the beginning of a beautiful and happy life.

'Just in the shallows,' he called after her.

She turned back. 'Of course.'

He'd taken the surfboard from the house – it was his dad's beach house and she could imagine him when he was young and lean, surfing the waves down here. He knew where his father stashed the spare keys so he didn't need to ask. They'd not been close in years and she knew he didn't entirely trust his son, or her for that matter.

She strode toward the water. Thinking about the last year. She hadn't put on as much weight as they say you do when you have a baby, but her hips were certainly wider now and she knew she looked different. She wore a one-piece and felt no self-consciousness. Even if it had been a Sunday in the middle of summer, and the sand had been packed with people, she still wouldn't have worried about what she looked like. Over the past few years, she'd learnt not to care what other people thought. In fact, sometimes she just wanted to do something different, *make a scene,* as if to invite the staring eyes of the public. You get over it. She looked back again, up the cliff toward the car park. The surfers had gone now, probably deciding the sea was a bit rough, the waves choppy and mostly unsurfable.

She looked to that quiet patch ahead, where a column of calm sea stretched out past the breakers. It was much steeper than she was expecting when she got to the water, and much cooler. Only a few feet in she was chest-deep, but it was nice, and diving under she was instantly refreshed, the chill of the water giving her a new energy. There was a gentle current too, but not so much that she couldn't keep her footing, except that now she could barely touch the ground.

She looked back toward the shore and realised she had drifted a little further than she'd meant to. She would just have to swim back. She was always fast at school, and she dug in, freestyle. A lifetime ago she was part of the Wesley College swim team where she'd spent early mornings dragging herself through the cold water of the pool. It was a slog, but the social side of it was fun, she'd made so many friends. They all drifted apart as they got older, though. Now she swam hard but the strength wasn't there in her arms like it used to be and when she looked up she was no closer to the sand. She was still drifting out. *Shit.*

*It's a rip.* The thought clotted in her chest. *I'm caught in a rip.* How could she not see it? The undertow continued to drag her, and battling against it had made her arms burn and chest ache for air. She tried to remember what you're supposed to do. Her dad's voice in her head. *Don't swim against it, swim parallel with the beach to get out of it.* She did, but it didn't seem to help, the undertow kept its hooks in and dragged her deeper and deeper.

'Help!' she screamed. 'Help!' Raising her hands seemed only to push her further under. *But isn't that what you're supposed to do?* she thought. Her heart slammed and she felt weak with the impossibility of the situation. It took just a second, a bad idea, and now she was in over her head. She surfaced, gasped, but water rushed into her mouth. She got her head up again and found herself caught in a set of huge, crushing waves. The swell tipped her, put her through a spin cycle, back arched and her legs thrown over her head. When the wave passed, she swam for the surface, her head screaming for air only to find she was swimming the wrong way, toward the sand. She righted herself, surfaced and sucked in a huge breath. The set of waves had passed, but more were coming, bending against the horizon. She threw her arms in the air again. 'Help!' she screamed, but before she could get the entire word out, the sea rushed into her mouth. She swallowed the briny swill, coughed, clawed hard for the surface. She was going to drown. She finally had all she wanted, a baby, a man who loved her and here she was, moments from dying.

Breaking back through the surface, she saw now that he was standing. He looked down into the basket, then back up toward the sea. What was he doing? Was he considering his options? He couldn't leave her out there to drown. *But he can't leave our son on the beach,* she thought, the panic rising. She knew in her heart that she wouldn't do it herself, she would stay with the baby, but he loved her. He loved them both so deeply. He had that instinct to do something crazy in moments of desperation. She'd seen him break a car window to save a dog trapped inside in the heat. He would come for her.

He bent, grabbed the surfboard and for just a second turned back and looked down at their son. He glanced off toward the boys with the frisbee; they were so far away but they'd realised something was off. Now he was running toward the water with the surfboard in his hands. He hit the sea in the area she was swept out from. He must have realised it was a rip after he saw how quickly it took her, and it would bring him all the way to her much faster. She could barely see the shore as another wave curled over her head and tumbled her. She swam for the surface, aching for breath, disoriented again, and when she got her head up another huge wave slammed her down. She surfaced once more, looked toward the beach and saw the boys standing on the sand watching her. *If I survive this,* she thought, *I will never ever be so reckless. I will always be there for him.* She was praying, she realised. She didn't know who she was praying to, but she was bargaining for her life. Religion was repellent in her worldview yet here she was begging some invisible entity to spare her.

She saw him again. He was paddling hard in her direction. She swam toward him and got to the surfboard.

'Just hold on,' he said, his voice hoarse from exertion. 'Squeeze the board tight, the waves will pull you in. Don't let go. No matter what, just hold on okay?'

'What about you?' she asked, shaken by the fear and the sudden cold. A cloud moved before the sun.

'Just go,' he said. 'I'll make it in.'

'No,' she said. 'No, I can't—'

'Just go! I'll be fine. The board won't carry us both.'

A wave came, it grabbed her and thrust her along, tipping the board up but she held on like he told her. Soon the wave was propelling her. Saltwater got up her nose, she slipped and felt the board slam against her cheek, but she held on. The wave died but not before cutting the distance to shore in half. She centred herself on the board and paddled, dragging herself through the calm patch. She was thinking about her brand-new perfect baby on the beach. He kept her going, kept her alive. She'd made a promise, she'd always be there for him. If she got through this, if she survived. Life, in this way, had changed for her. Another wave came, this time it was smaller, all snarling white. It didn't thrust her along, but it towed her off the back of the whitewash toward the shore. The nose of the board ground against the sand. She stood, her body trembling. She scrambled over the sand, leaving the board in the shallows, and the boys who'd been throwing the frisbee came running over, helped her up the beach and wrapped her in a towel.

'Are you okay?' one of them asked. 'You're bleeding.'

She fought them off, pushing away as she staggered across the sand on aching legs.

'I'm fine,' she said, still breathless and trembling. Her hand came to her cheek and when she looked at her palm she was surprised to see blood. A lot of blood. She remembered knocking it on the board, but it didn't feel painful, it must just be a scratch. Or maybe it is bad. Maybe the cold of the water had numbed her or the adrenaline had chased the pain from her consciousness. She turned back to the sea and could see him struggling against the drag of the waves, still out there where she'd been. He was out so deep. A fist opened and closed in her sternum, and she felt lightheaded and desperate, like she might faint. She sent another prayer out into the ether. *Please, please bring him in. Please save him like he saved me.*

'Has someone called for help?' she said, her voice charged with desperation. 'Have you got a phone? Why aren't you calling for help?'

'Our friend ran back up to the car,' one if the boys said. 'He's calling an ambulance.'

*He never should have left the baby alone on the beach*, she thought, rushing up the sand toward her son now. *What if they'd both drowned? What then?* She exhaled.

She knew in that moment that something had changed inside. She'd always be there for her baby. *Always.* She turned back and watched as he struggled against the power of the ocean. He'd saved her life. Now she prayed again that he would make it back in, that they would all survive this.

# PART ONE

# ONE

YOU MIGHT HAVE hated me at one point in time. Lots of people have. It's fine, really.

You *have* to get used to it in that line of work. We were up there with parking wardens, traffic police. The hatred usually only lasted for a minute or two, and by the time people got through to the arrival gate they'd forgotten about me and I'd forgotten about them, but there was always another person ready, passport in hand, dragging their suitcases with dead-eyed, thinly disguised contempt. It was the ones coming home from holidays who were the worst. They should've been in a good mood, with their sun tans and Bintang singlets, kids with braided hair, but they were all going back to their nine-to-fives, traffic, cooking their own meals, school.

You might have seen me or perhaps not. People didn't really see us at the airport, it's like we'd already been replaced by machines.

They sort of looked through us as we probed with questions, watching for *tells*. If I believed you, you went straight through; if I doubted you or I didn't like you, you went into the long queue for additional screening. It could be the difference between making a connecting flight, seeing your family for Christmas, or missing out. That's why people hated me, and I forgave them. Forgave. Past tense now, you know, *before* all this. When I still had a job. In the pre-virus world. The virus feels like a boundary between the country of the present and the country of the past. Those robotic scanners were sweeping through the terminals anyway, it was only a matter of time before they replaced us. The break in international travel just seemed to accelerate things. With more scanners and fewer people, they could process travellers just as quickly with a lighter wage bill. Machines that read body language and flag travellers exhibiting suspicious behaviour without all the *human* biases. I did love that job though. The colleagues, the hours, the time between rushes of travellers when I could just stand there and think.

Redundancy was offered after the second wave, then it was mandatory after the third. Six months' wages paid out after eleven years of hard work, but I can't complain really. So many others had it so much worse. Now the fourth wave is here. This new vaccine-resistant strain of the virus has arrived, a cluster was detected north of the city. I saw it on the news this afternoon and my first thought was *not again*. My second was *I hope Samuel has seen this*.

I'm still thinking about him from where I sit out in the afternoon sun. It's warm for early spring. I'm in my usual spot, on our balcony overlooking Punt Road, the busiest street in the city, and it's even busier now with the news of the lockdown. The two outbound lanes are choked up with city dwellers fleeing for their holiday homes in coastal enclaves. No such privilege here.

In lockdown, we're allowed out to exercise but most of the time I'm happy enough just staying in. I'm at that point in my life when I know I'll never be in the shape I was in my twenties. I'm hurtling toward menopause and I've decided to do what I need to do to keep myself happy. My therapist helped me see that starving myself and resisting the things that make me happy is unhealthy and being a thin, teetotalling, meditation guru seems nice but that's not me. So, I like to drink the occasional glass of wine and smoke a few cigarettes a day and spend time with my son. If and when a man enters my life it's usually on my terms. Samuel always comes first.

I go to his bedroom now and check again, as though impossibly he might not be out at all. He could still be there asleep under the covers after a late-night cramming and maybe I've just missed him all day. That hope fades instantly. No sign of him, just an unmade bed, sheets tangled, half on the bed, half on the floor. That large poster of Nietzsche on the wall, staring down, mildly judgemental with that bushy moustache and inscrutable gaze. *Nietzsche,* all the smartest people in history seem to only need one name. *Einstein, Da Vinci, Shakespeare.* I don't know a thing about Nietzsche, I just know he was a philosopher and his ideas are much too clever for me. That's a bit like everything with my Samuel, he has a big brain with bigger ideas and try as I might to keep up, I always fail to really understand. His monitor is in the corner on his desk, but his laptop is gone. The room floods with light when I sweep the curtains open. I see some dirty clothes on the floor, and a hair tie – not his – on the bedstand.

Our bedrooms are side by side and symmetrical. The living room is sizeable for an apartment, although I always had dreams of saving up, buying something bigger, maybe a house with a back yard, but any money I did save went straight back into Samuel's studies, and without a job it's unlikely I'll ever have enough to leave this place. It's tough as a single mother, it's tougher still as an *unemployed* single mother. But that's okay. We like it here, and one day Samuel is going to make a lot of money. Then he will start his own family on a nice big family block with a two-storey house, a Labrador, maybe even a small pool to cool off in. There will be a granny flat out the back for me and I'll babysit the kids when he and his wife, whoever she may be, are too busy or need a break. Short of winning the lottery, it's unlikely I'll be moving out of this apartment anytime soon, but a woman can dream of the future. Five, ten years, who knows what our lives will look like. So many young people are making so much money these days. And like I said, Samuel's much, much smarter than me and *definitely* smarter than Marko.

My husband became a different man the day he decided to get behind the wheel drunk; eventually he'd stop drinking altogether. But things really fell apart for us a year later, that day at the beach with the huge waves. It's eighteen years ago and Samuel was just a newborn but it's hard not to view that day as the beginning of the end of our marriage. We were together three more tough years, we tried to make it work, but we were both drifting. During that time I began to realise that I cared much more about Samuel than I did about him. And Marko realised I just wasn't the type of woman he wanted to spend the rest of his life with.

Marko got what he wanted in the end, a simple normal, easy family. It seemed he'd only been with his new girlfriend ten minutes before they were engaged, and she was swollen with their first kid. When I went into labour, he was working. He turned up halfway through. I suppose it didn't help that labour started six weeks early. I'm sure he was there for *her*, his new wife. They probably skipped the years of *trying*, the miscarriages and desperation.

Like I said, that day at the beach is what ruined things with me and Marko, but it bound me so tightly to Samuel – I never, ever want to go through that again. Anything could have happened. It was the most intense emotional experience, the fear and anxiety, the pure unfiltered relief. I didn't leave the house at all for weeks after that. I just wanted to spend all my time with him. It wasn't until he was at school that I started working again, then I saw him a little less. Especially when I had night shifts and he'd stay at his father's.

Now Marko is Mr Outdoors with those three nauseatingly toothy blonde girls. I guess it's much easier for men to reinvent themselves, abandon their families and start afresh.

I know I should leave it for him to do, but I make Samuel's bed, collect the washing from the floor. That's when I notice something. I stop, stoop down and pick up one of his anthropology textbooks, propping his dirty clothes against my hip. It's from one of his classes. There's a bookmark a third of the way through. I also find the empty packaging of a nasal swab. It must be from one of those rapid swab tests. I wonder when he did it?

I take his washing through to the bathroom where the washing machine is. His favourite white shirt is there in the pile. I take it to my nose to check it's been worn, and I can smell him. I toss the shirt in with the rest and set the washing machine going.

Back outside, I sit with my phone in my hand and begin an afternoon of what I know will be scrolling through social media, tumbling headlong down the infinite rabbit hole. I've got a new follower, *BlueRazoo11*. I never get new followers, maybe it's an old friend from school, or someone I'd worked with at the airport. I check out their profile, just photos on a farm. Some of dogs, or sheep, an old pond. Mostly animals, in static poses. Their eyes beady with the tell-tale sign of taxidermy.

I feel something brush against my ankle.

'Hey, Moo,' I say, looking down at our black and white cat. 'You hungry?' I reach and scratch between her ears. Moo laces herself around my legs.

Moo is eleven. Samuel named her. Taking one look when she was a kitten, my ten-year-old son said, 'Can we call him Cow?'

'We could. Any other ideas?'

16

'Moo?' he was laughing as he said it, then I started laughing and just like that we had a name.

I eye the time, it's just after three now as the afternoon sun begins its descent toward the cityscape and the horizon beyond. I call Samuel again, holding the phone between my ear and shoulder as I pour cat biscuits into Moo's bowl. Third time today I've called. This time it goes straight to voicemail.

Today he was going to study at the state library with her, Jessica. Which makes sense, given he took his backpack and his laptop. Then he was heading to see his father this afternoon. Not to stay with him, just to see him. That was the plan, but when I messaged Marko, he'd not heard from him either. There's a distant alarm sounding, not there out in the city but inside. A hum of anxiety. I push it away but it's still there throbbing in my chest. Something feels off.

I just wish Marko was more help. When he met Christine, she instantly replaced me, and a few years later the girls replaced Samuel, in the same way those automatic machines at the airport replaced half my colleagues. We are all being replaced one way or another. You might not think you're next, you probably think you're safe because you and your job are special. Then before you know it, you're out the door with a redundancy cheque and a sorry handshake. You'll land in a job market for what recruiters call *digital natives*.

When Marko left, I started smoking again. He always hated it. He was half the reason I stopped, but after he left, I went to the corner store and bought the first pack of cigarettes I'd smoked since I was a teenager. Marlboros – I never used to smoke Marlboros – I got through the entire pack and two bottles of wine, imagining what it would be like to tip myself off the balcony into the traffic below. Samuel was a toddler then, he kept me going.

Whenever I think about the life we could have had, whenever I get sad, I sit out here. In the last lockdown Samuel found me on this balcony with tears running down my face like I was sixteen again in the Espy Hotel bathrooms with my fake ID and layers of poorly applied make-up. Back then it was a punk gig. I'd been looking forward to it for months, but some creep grabbed me in a not entirely unfriendly way but with enough force to just set me off crying. This was of course pre-#metoo. My high school friend found me that time, and dragged me back onto the dancefloor, putting a vodka Red Bull in my hand. With my head wedged on the inside of her elbow, she bent and kissed me on the temple.

'You'll get used to it!' she yelled over the music. 'It happens sometimes at gigs. Ignore him and he'll go away.'

That was Cassie. We were never that close but she was a nice girl and we swam together. She got into drugs a couple of years later and that was where we parted company.

'Come on inside, Mum,' Samuel had told me that night on the balcony.

'No,' I slurred. 'I want to watch the cars.' It was soon after the redundancy, when the lockdowns just kept rolling on and on. I was missing my mum and mourning a life I never really had.

'Well, I'll drink with you if you get off this bloody balcony and put the cigarettes away. Let's watch some TV.'

That was what Samuel did. He would comfort me. I always raised him to be kind and above all else honest. After Marko's night of drunk driving, I knew firsthand how septic lies and secrets could be. Secrets destroy relationships. I raised him to know he could always trust me, he could tell me anything and so long as he always did the right thing and told the truth, nothing would go wrong.

I sit out on the balcony now and look over my corner of the world.

*Wherever you are at eight tonight, you must stay there,* that was the directive. *We need to get back on top of this thing, bring the numbers down. Strain four vaccinations will be ready in three weeks.* I take up my phone, looking through the cracked screen.

I text him again.

*You have to be home by eight tonight – they've brought the curfew back. Let me know asap when you'll get in.*

I haven't heard back from Marko either, other than the one message he sent a couple of hours ago, three words and a treasonous question mark: *Samuel turned up?*

By the time four o'clock ticks around the pebble of doubt in my stomach has grown to a stone. *Why hasn't he messaged me or answered my calls?* I allow another question to creep into my skull and take hold of my brain: *what if he doesn't come back in time?* It's valid. It's a real anxiety. *Lockdown wasn't as good for him as it was for you last time,* I think. Human brains do this, they try to tell you the truth even if you don't want to hear it: either you win and you block it out, or your brain wins and the truth gets you in its teeth and doesn't let go.

I switch the TV on, the news channel, and turn it up loud enough that I can hear it out on the balcony. I watch the entrance of the building down below, hoping to see him. I don't know why I put the news on, perhaps to hear if there was a delay on the trains, or maybe they'll announce that mobile phone coverage is down. Maybe the talking heads on ABC News can answer why I haven't heard from my son but all they're talking about is the lockdown, the rules, the press conference from the state leader. I check my phone again.

I've always resisted social media, it's perfectly fine to scroll, I do it most of the day, but I never post. I'm not on a flawless sunny beach, I'm not contorting myself into impossible yoga poses, I'm not particularly beautiful or funny and I can't do a make-up tutorial. I've posted a few photos over the years but I find the idea of opening up my personal life to the anonymous world of the internet both pointless and uncomfortable.

Samuel is different. Once upon a time he was a vlogger, posting daily updates about his life on YouTube to his small but faithful group of subscribers. Each vlog would amass a couple of hundred views and a few comments. He was mostly posting videos of himself talking about school, his life, what he wanted to do in the future, but occasionally he would talk about politics, climate change or things he would alter about the world. I imagined his channel blowing up, he was so charismatic on the screen. Then one day he grew out of it.

On Samuel's YouTube channel there are no new posts since 2020. I watch a few of them, skipping through the years and seeing the way his face changed as the early teen puppy fat shed, as he went through puberty and emerged the other side a handsome, confident young man. I can see videos that he has recently watched and liked. There's a Radiohead song, and now I can see he's left a comment. I click it and find that it's got thirty-four likes. *What if the truth doesn't set you free? What if the truth is the cage?* My chest tightens. It seems a contradiction of the one thing I thought he stood for, the thing I've always tried to instil. *No secrets.*

I think about Marko all those years ago, one of the last nights he drank alcohol, when his life changed forever. I hear the crunch of the car. It's a secret that I'd agreed to keep until the grave . . . can a secret be inherited? What if Samuel overheard something, or found some evidence? No, I tell myself. No, everything is fine. He'll be home before night. There's nothing to worry about.

# SAMUEL

I'VE BEEN WAITING for half an hour at the cafe, thinking I might have been stood up, and I can't send a message because my mobile battery is flat. Maybe I'm at the wrong place? Maybe I got the wrong time? There isn't anything I can do about it now. I left my laptop at Jessica's – I'll be heading back there soon – and without my university work or any technology to distract me, I'm stuck here alone with my thoughts. There is a lot going through my mind but I know this is the right thing to do, so why then am I thinking about how much this might hurt the ones I love most? Especially Mum. She would never expect this of me.

I try to distract myself from these thoughts. I think about Immanuel Kant, the philosopher. His view of truth was absolute. He believed there was no such thing as a moral lie. All lies were amoral. And without lies, without deception, there's really no need for secrets. This is a bit like what Mum always told me. Secrets and lies destroy relationships, but what if the alternative is worse? What if a secret or a lie can save you?

Now, as I reach out and sip my drink, I see the chair pulled out across the table and someone sits down.

I look up.

'I was worried you weren't going to make it,' I say, with my biggest smile but it's forced. Something still doesn't feel right. Nerves surge in my chest. Maybe I shouldn't be here at all.

# TWO

I JUST STARE at the background of my phone, that dopey picture of us from the *Thriller*-themed restaurant. All werewolves in red jackets, then us at the table with our food and the wait staff around the booth grinning. It was my birthday. He didn't have to do it, I know he hates stuff like that, but he took me there because I've always seen the ads on TV. I'd wondered if it would be any good; the food wasn't great but we had fun. He can be a bit goofy when he's away from his friends, just us two, like he's my little boy again.

I think about that YouTube comment again. It could be tongue in cheek. Who knows, I've always struggled to decipher online teen slang. On TikTok I find his profile photo. It's with her, Jessica. That photo where he has his arm around her shoulders.

It's a selfie, and she's smiling, or rather making herself smile. Here's how to spot a fake: check for bottom teeth visibility. If you can see the bottom teeth, it's probably not real. Step two: look at the eyes. If the eyes are not closing a little, or are not creased at the edges, then it's *not* a real smile. Jessica misses on both counts, yet Samuel has the biggest *I just won the lottery* grin you'll find. See her body language now. He is pulling her closer, but she angles away from him at the hips. She is letting him hold her rather than wanting to be held. I'm trained to spot these things, and I've always seen the signs that there is something off. She's nervous, she's concealing something – it's written all over her face whenever I see her.

Moo starts to clean herself on the dining table. I lock my phone, place it beside the ashtray and try to forget about it.

As the day continues to tick by and the sun descends lower and lower, the stone in my gut grows bigger. Between puffs on my next cigarette, I chew my thumbnail, watching down on the street, searching for that lanky shape of him. Any moment, he'll get off the tram and come bounding toward the apartment building with his satchel bag over his shoulder. I call him again. It goes straight to voicemail.

'Hi, you've reached Sam's phone. Leave a message and I'll get back to you.'

I exhale, find my breath shaky. *He's nineteen years old, he can look after himself. He will make it home.*

'Hi Samuel, call me please. I hope you've seen the news about the lockdown tonight. I'm worried about you and if you're caught out late, we can't afford the fine. Not to mention the possibility of spending a night in a jail cell. Please call so I know you're okay.'

When I hang up, I just stare at the screen, that photo from the *Thriller* restaurant. If I keep watching it, I won't miss the call when he eventually dials back. Still time passes. Six o'clock now. Then six-fifteen. At six-thirty, I call again. No answer. I try his father. It almost rings out before he picks up.

'Lou,' he says slow and flat, like he's already sick of this conversation.

'Is he there?'

'Who? Samuel?'

'Yes, Samuel. Who else?'

'No, he's not here.'

'He was supposed to be visiting you today?'

'Well, he never came by, why don't you call *him*?'

'Oh, that's a grand idea, why didn't I think of that?'

'I'm hanging up, Lou. I don't want you getting snarky.'

I let the breath drain out of my chest. *Stay calm, Lou.* 'Our son might be missing, Marko.'

He makes an ugly, dismissive hissing sound. 'Missing? He was there this morning, right? He's probably with Jessica.'

'Maybe, but he's got to be home by eight. I can't afford a bloody fine.'

'Is this really about a fine?'

'What the hell is that supposed to mean?'

He clears his throat. 'The boy is an adult.'

'So? What's that got to do with it?'

He lets a few seconds pass. I can hear him breathing. I'm so used to the sounds he makes, his frustrated breath, the huff of it. Or his laugh, almost inaudible – just quick exhales through the nose. And those mornings, years ago in our late teens, when I'd watch the rise and fall of his hairy chest while he slept. Seems an age ago now. He speaks again. 'Maybe he's planning on staying with Jessica.'

And just like that, he's aired that deep apprehension. I feel winded. An unwanted thought that lives where I keep all those anxieties: *He's outgrown me.*

'No,' I say to myself as much as Marko. 'No, you don't understand. He lives here, all of his stuff is here.' I want to say *He loves it here,* but I don't want to sound delusional. Just logical. This man, I remind myself, subscribes to a pure ideal about logic. Everything has to make sense even when it doesn't.

'Yes but . . .' A pause. 'Well, I hear you don't like the girl. Before you jump down my throat, that's a little bit from Samuel, plus my own intuition.'

'Marko,' I say, trying to keep my voice measured. 'I'm telling you something is wrong. His phone is off. He was supposed to visit you today. He's supposed to be back tonight and since they announced this lockdown, well, he's not been heard from.'

'At seven-fifty-five, he'll walk in the door, and you'll yell at him, and he'll explain what happened. Then he will apologise, and all will be forgiven.'

'And if he doesn't?'

'Well, he did say something last time I saw him, when the first few cases of the new variant were announced.'

'Go on?' I find my body tensing with anticipation.

'He said that next time he was thinking about staying with Jessica, if there was another lockdown. And I asked him if he had told you that, and he said he would, but not yet. He wasn't sure how you would take it.'

'You're telling me this now?'

'I didn't think it was so important. I thought he must have mentioned it to you.'

'No,' I say. 'He would have still sent me a text message.'

'His battery might be flat.'

'Can you stop being so flippant. Are you not a little worried?'

'No,' he says. 'Frankly, I'm not worried. I think it's safe to assume he's a little keener on being locked inside with his girlfriend than his alcoholic mother.'

*Why do you need to drop 'alcoholic' in there?* 'You prick,' I say. 'If I am an alcoholic, you made me one, so don't you dare throw that in my face.'

'Ha,' he says. 'I made you one, did I? That's rich, Lou. I've barely touched a drop of alcohol in over fifteen years.'

'And why is that, Marko?'

I can almost see him down the phone, that dark hair that is now speckled with grey. 'I know you're not saying what I think you're saying. You agreed, *we* agreed.'

'That I wouldn't tell anyone about the . . .' I pause, I know I shouldn't go any further but I'm still hot from the *alcoholic* comment, '. . . the cyclist.' I hear a door slam down the line.

My face feels hot against the phone. I've overstepped. Finally, he exhales. 'I'm hanging up now. I suggest you clear your head and calm down before you speak with him next,' he says. 'And don't *ever* even hint at what *we* did, not just me, Lou.'

Then he's gone and it takes me a moment to remove the phone from my ear. What if he's right? What if Samuel really is with *her?* I hear his words again in my mind. *I think it's safe to assume he's a little keener on being locked inside with his girlfriend than his alcoholic mother.*

So I like a drink – who doesn't? He knows nothing about addiction, the good little teetotalling saint. I saw addiction firsthand, well sort of; Cassie from high school was an addict. Plus we lived for a brief period off Victoria Street near the city, where from time to time you'd see people shooting up in alleyways, or behind retail stores. That's what addiction looks like. That's just it, heroin is different to alcohol. I saw Cassie years later; she'd been in and out of rehab. She came right for a couple of years, then I saw on Facebook she had plunged right back into that world. That's different to my occasional glasses of wine in the afternoon. Marko doesn't know anything about me or my life, but I know about his.

I know what he did and if his secret came out, his perfect little life would come crashing down.

I continue to sit and wait for Samuel. With each passing minute, my chest feels tighter and tighter.

# THREE

IF IT HADN'T gotten so cold, I might have stayed out there on the balcony all night, my nails chewed to the quick, endlessly scrolling social media while I waited to hear from Samuel. I drag a chair over to the window to continue watching the street below from the warmth of the living room. When Moo leaps up onto my lap, I shoo her away. She's surly but I'm too anxious to keep still enough for her to perch there. The TV is on, the news running scenes from grocery store queues of panic buyers, the army out in their fatigues monitoring social distancing. Soon the late news comes on and after that, around midnight, an old Western. I doze off in the chair, waking minutes or perhaps hours later, to reach for my phone again and check if he has tried to contact me. The cold dark night outside presses its nose up to the glass.

Each time I wake, my caesarean scar itches. Most people don't believe in anything supernatural, but it's always been this way, a tingle in the scar tissue whenever I'm worried about him.

'Where's your human, Moo? Where is he?' But Moo is still grumpy at me and glances over with raw contempt. I doze off again.

When I wake in the morning, sunlight streams in through the windows. It's far too early and my mouth tastes like I ate an ashtray in my sleep. At some stage in the night, I've made my way from the chair to the couch. I pull myself up and go to his room. I see the bed I made for him yesterday, perfectly neat. He didn't sneak home while I slept, he hasn't been here all along, hiding. My heart sinks. It's like he's vanished, sucked up from the face of the earth. I clean the kitchen, put the wine bottle in the recycling bin, empty the ashtray, now full of water from the rain overnight, the cigarette butts floating like the drowned at sea. It's good, cathartic work tidying up, readying everything for when he comes home. So he stayed the first night at Jessica's. That's no big deal, so long as he gets in touch today.

Looks-wise, Samuel is tall – more on the lanky side than athletic, but good-looking. That's not just me seeing him through a mother's eyes. That's me looking at the evidence – the endless string of girls who have always hung around, who follow him on YouTube and social media. He was popular at school and he cares about other people. So, of course, his first love was going to be pretty. But she is also smart. Jessica is studying something to do with the classics ... history, ancient civilisations and *religious* studies. Hardly my cup of tea, although it seems to interest Samuel, but then again *everything* interests Samuel. That's where they met, actually. In a class. They found themselves in a study group in first year. Cupid's arrow hit its mark.

I told Samuel to invite her for dinner and I found out all I could about her before we met, yet I was unprepared for just how nauseatingly polite she was. Polite in a way a robot would be trained to be. It was the little things she said and the looks she gave the food that suggested the courtesy was all an act.

I don't normally cook much for us, and what I do cook you would hardly call fine dining, but I made my best spaghetti bolognaise that night. My mum's recipe. The sauce conjured out of mince, a bag of tomatoes, onions, some fresh herbs, olive oil, red wine and spices. It's been a favourite in our house from when Samuel was a fussy toddler who would only eat meals with tomato sauce. The table was set, and candles lit and dribbling wax. Gentle music played through the speaker beneath the TV.

She arrived early, while I was still cooking. 'Hi,' I said when she came through the door. I offered my hand. 'I'm Lou, Sam's mum.'

'Oh, it's such a pleasure to finally meet you,' she said, a saccharine note in her voice as she pulled me into an unwelcome hug. I could feel the thin bones of her spine. Too slender, too pretty. I learnt in high school not to trust women like this.

'Oh, you're a hugger,' I noted.

'Of course, I feel like I already know you,' she said, releasing me and stepping back. 'Samuel has told me everything about you.

I've been waiting for so long but it's hard to organise these things, isn't it?'

'Yeah, likewise,' I said. 'Samuel's told me all about you too.' This was a year ago, between lockdowns, when they had only been together for a couple of months. 'Now make yourself at home, I'm almost finished in the kitchen. I hope you're hungry.'

'Did you need any help, Ma?' Samuel offered.

'No,' I said. 'But why don't you get Jessica a glass of wine?'

'Oh, I'm not much of a wine drinker, water will be fine.'

I tried to meet her smile. Blonde hair with pale blue eyes and fair skin that would have taken a beating in the Australian summer sun as a kid.

'Sure.'

She wore a pale dress and only a little make-up. The fact she didn't want a glass of wine made me somehow trust her less. What is it about teetotallers that makes me suspicious? They're almost always ex-alcoholics, like Marko, or holier-than-thou wellness types. But she was neither.

When I served dinner at the table, I half-expected her to say grace. She simply said, 'I am so grateful for this meal. It's not easy finding a nice hearty home-cooked meal in this city.'

'No,' I agreed. 'So you grew up in the country?'

'I did, on a farm of sorts.'

'Oh,' I said, sipping my wine. 'What did you farm?'

'Sorry?'

'Dairy cattle, lamb?'

'Well, we grew most of our own food. My brothers and dad butchered and hunted any meat we had. Eggs from the chickens, milk from the cows.'

'Good lifestyle out there?'

'It is. I was so lucky to grow up with my family. My father was always good to us and worked so hard. It was really different to the city,' she said. I watched as she turned her fork through her food, studying the knotted spaghetti as if it was something I'd trawled up out of the shower drain.

'And what did your parents do for work?'

'Well, they raised us,' she said. 'My father is a minister. And there was always work at home on the farm.'

'He's religious?'

'Yes,' she says. 'Many more people are out in the country. The city is different. So big and busy but also not a place where people have much belief in anything.'

'And you?'

'Sorry?'

'Are you religious?'

She sat staring at her fork for a moment. 'Um, yeah,' she said, a closed-lip smile between mouthfuls of spaghetti. 'Yeah, I'd say I still believe.'

'In what?'

'In God. Um, I . . .' She clicked her tongue, frowning.

'Mum,' Samuel said.

'What?'

'Let's talk about something else.'

I found myself wondering if the two of them had had sex yet. I supposed not, depending on what flavour of God and what *I still believe* meant.

'And when are you meeting Jessica's parents?' I said to Samuel.

'I don't know. When I'm invited to meet them,' he said, eyeing Jessica conspiratorially.

'I don't know if you're ready for my family, you might run for the hills.'

'Any scary ex-boyfriends?' I said, teasing her, trying to get some banter going.

She smiled. 'No, no ex-boyfriends buried in the backyard.'

At the end of the evening, when things were all wrapped up, I went to bed and left them watching TV on the couch. I wasn't about to kick her out and I expected she was planning on staying – after all, she had brought a small bag, probably containing a change of clothes and a toothbrush. Samuel had had other girlfriends over, and Marko cared so little that I'm sure Samuel could do whatever he wanted when he was at his father's.

That night, at around midnight, when I heard his bedroom door close and the murmur of voices, I wondered if the walls were thick enough for what might transpire. My question was soon answered when the sound of her giggling gave way at first to silence, then the movement of sheets and blankets, short breaths, the faintest whining of the bed. I put headphones on to block it out. But then came her moaning. Sudden and loud, the bellow of an animal in pain or ecstasy, then it was gone. I took the headphones off, as if to reassure myself I'd heard correctly. *What sort of girl would do that? Make that sort of sound, knowing her boyfriend's mum was in the next room?* It was almost as though she wanted to be heard – she let it out to mark her territory – then Samuel had quickly covered her mouth or had stopped doing whatever had stimulated it. I felt gross, complicit almost. My boy. Doing that. It's not something a mother enjoys imagining, but there I was, wide-eyed with equal parts horror and disgust, a cocktail of revulsion. I had half a mind to go knock on his door but couldn't bring myself to do it.

In the morning, she was gone. Slipping from the apartment without a trace that she'd been there at all. I found Samuel eating his bowl of Nutri-Grain on the couch, with a book propped open across his lap. A little colour came to his cheeks when he saw me.

'Morning, Mum.'

'Morning,' I said. I wanted to mention what happened, but I didn't want to make him relive it. The shame was obvious, and that was punishment enough.

'Jessica gone?'

'She had class and needed to pick some books up from her apartment.'

'Right,' I said. 'Well, it was nice to finally meet her.' Then I let a beat pass. 'I hope she doesn't convert you.'

He didn't smile.

'To God, or . . . whatever.'

'Oh,' he said, turning on that 10,000-watt grin. 'Unlikely. I don't think she's really that religious anymore.'

Weeks later when I caught up with Viv and the girls for wine, I replayed the story and they all cackled.

Viv said, 'You probably did the same with Marko when you were young.'

I made a vomiting face. 'She was just weird, you know. There is something off with her. I can't place it, but I sense it.'

'God-botherers, all hypocrites usually, but she sounds nice enough. Maybe your son has converted her to atheism through the powers of his bedroom dark arts,' Christina said.

'It's probably a power move, establish herself in your home,' Janet suggested.

'Well,' Viv said. 'I don't know about you guys, but she sounds like a little psychopath to me. Just from everything you've told me, Lou.'

I was glad for Viv's friendship most of the time, but especially then. Finally some support, confirmation that it wasn't all in my head. That sort of behaviour is pathological. I'd be sending Jessica through for additional screening at the airport, without missing a beat.

'I agree. She's no good. Not for my boy. I only hope he grows out of it. I hope I don't have to have a talk with him. I hope he meets a nice, *quiet* girl instead.'

# FOUR

MY THERAPIST HAS tried to help me understand why I feel anxious and, at times, guilty. But there are some secrets – Marko's secret, the car crash – that I can't share with her. I try to be completely honest but if I revealed the source of my guilt, Marko would probably kill me, and we'd likely both end up in jail. Today, I try not to catastrophise, instead opting to carry on as if nothing is amiss. I wait to hear from my son, but I don't sit there staring at my phone. *A watched pot never boils.*

I make lunch, croissants with tomatoes and cheese. When my doorbell rings I know it's my grocery order and find it there, waiting for me at the door to the building.

The video call with the girls starts at 4 pm. We all went to school together, except Viv who was in the UK but fits into our group so seamlessly you'd think we'd known her forever. Video calls can be awkward, especially when there's a small delay and lots of people. Sometimes it feels a little like everybody is trying to walk through the same door all at once. But in past lockdowns I had the most fun with these girls, and we all dragged each other through the hard weeks. We got used to communicating over the screen, getting drunk together, sharing odd gossip and filling the hours with mindless chat.

Frances is giving us a review of a dating show she has been watching on Netflix. We all laugh as she describes the filled lips and fake boobs. When Debbie asks what Samuel is doing, I freeze. I don't know what to say.

'Oh, actually Samuel isn't here.'

'He's out exercising, or getting food?'

'No,' I say. 'Not that I know of.'

An awkward pause. 'Well, where is he, pray tell?' Viv says *pray tell* a lot and, with her British accent, it gives her an air of sophistication that all goes out the window after a couple of Friday afternoon chardonnays.

'He's at his girlfriend's. He's staying there,' I say. The words seem to leave a trail of acid that stings my throat. I force a smile but when I see my tiny, pixelated face on the screen, I look sad. How to spot a fake smile: visible lower teeth, no creases around the eyes.

'Oh,' Janet says.

'Well, that's good,' Brenda adds. 'Freedom. Maybe you could have a visitor of your own. Intimate partners are allowed.'

She might be talking about Steve, the plumber who came home with me after a date at the pub one night when Samuel was staying at Marko's place. He gave me fifteen minutes of mediocre sex before dissolving onto me, almost suffocating us both. After a few moments he rolled off, saying, 'I better get going. Work in the morning.' I'd not heard from him in a month. Hardly qualifies as an *intimate partner*.

'No, it's fine. It's a good thing, I needed to cut the apron strings.'

'And you've warmed to her?' Viv asks now.

I exhale, thinking about how to say this.

'That is answer enough,' someone jokes.

'No—' I say.

'Oh, you should have seen the look you gave.'

I see all their smiling faces on the screen. I try to shape a smile myself, but it feels like someone has taped my cheeks back.

'Honestly,' I say. 'She's fine. She's perfectly fine.' I know it's unconvincing, but it seems to shift the conversation along and soon we are talking about something else. I find my mind wandering to the top drawer in my bedroom. Not to the pink rechargeable wand that replaced male company in my life, but to a piece of paper. On that piece of paper is a prescription my doctor wrote for antidepressants. I've held off; I never saw myself as the type of person who needs meds, but my therapist told me it can be a good way to weather the tough periods. I decide I will fill the script. I can't do this alone. I can't face the isolation, or the fact that my son has chosen Jessica over me. I will continue to see my therapist online but it's not cheap. I can only afford it once a month.

When Samuel does finally call me back, or messages, I won't be angry; I will simply be relieved – I can't push him further away. There was a day a few weeks ago when he was moody with me after I'd come into his room. He'd snapped his laptop closed.

'What do you want?'

'I was just seeing what you're up to in here.'

'Uni stuff,' he'd said. I noticed the bags under his eyes. He was studying too hard, and I knew he was becoming interested in cryptocurrencies. It was all a little over my head, but he seemed to know what he was talking about.

'What stuff?'

He rolled his eyes. 'Stuff you wouldn't understand. Just some papers I've got to write.'

I stood there, gobsmacked. *Where had my little boy gone?* 'Samuel,' I snapped. 'Don't speak to me that way.'

'Sorry,' he said. 'Is there anything else? I've got work to do.'

'No,' I said, backing out of the room.

I stood outside his door listening as he opened the laptop again and started tapping away. He had a special way of making me feel very lonely when he was like that, just how Marko had.

I don't think kids really understand what it is like to raise them. I don't think they have any idea of the sacrifices parents make. Samuel won't understand until he goes through it all himself.

I think about when I gave birth. Marko was late, arriving afterward. Then in the following months he was back working a lot, sometimes out at night seeing appointments while I was in the house dripping milk, feeling the constant stress and anxiety. I couldn't sleep, I was always worried. The maternal and child health nurse told me early on, 'Nap when the baby naps.'

But even that I failed at, because for the first year at least, whenever Samuel was silent, I would constantly worry that something was wrong. I would assume he had stopped breathing and go in and check, resting my finger near his nose to feel the tickle of his breath. Sometimes he would wake, and begin to howl and I would soothe him, feeling both relieved and exhausted anew. I had nightmares about him dying.

I go to the kitchen and make a coffee. I take my phone and find myself checking his social media again. I go back to YouTube, to that comment he left.

*What if the truth doesn't set you free? What if the truth is the cage?*

This time I click the responses under his comment, to see how people reacted to it. One sticks out.

*That's heavy. Speaking from experience?*

He responded. Reading his words causes the breath to freeze in my throat.

*I'm sorry. I don't want to talk about my daddy issues with a stranger online.*

The truth. *Daddy issues.* This interaction is from a few weeks ago. *What do you know, Samuel?*

Could this be about Marko, then, and that night he got behind the wheel after five pints? I still remember the engagement party we were at. It was for people I've not seen in fifteen years and during the speeches they announced they were pregnant to roars of joy from everyone there, except us. We'd been trying for a couple of years by that stage. Their announcement was a good enough reason for Marko and me to get drunk and reckless. We didn't think about the potential consequences. We didn't know I'd fall pregnant just weeks later. We didn't know Samuel would come.

Is that what this is about? Could Samuel know? The phone dings. It's a message from Samuel. My breath catches in my throat.

*Hey Mum, I feel so bad and I am really sorry I didn't get onto you yesterday. Phone issues, I won't bore you with the details. As you've probably guessed I was with Jessica all day and when the news came through, I decided to lockdown here. It was so hard last time and you could do with a little of your own space. I'll call you in the next day or two.*

There it is. The truth of the matter. He's clearly thought a lot about this message. It almost doesn't seem like him. Too formal, and not his style of messaging. A sliver of me, the tiniest, sharpest part of me, preferred it when I didn't know where he was. At least then there was a chance he wasn't with her. But of course, it could have been much worse too. It's not just the fact he's staying there, it's the fact he knows it would hurt me – that's why there's none of his usual banter.

# SAMUEL

THERE'S A THOUGHT experiment one of the professors at university talked about once. This is the scenario: you are sitting in a comfortable windowless room, beside an open fire with an old man, or perhaps an old woman – someone you trust and like. You talk for hours; the conversation is interesting, and you feel affection for this person who has been nothing but kind and cordial. But you soon discover that the door is locked from the outside and there is no way to leave. The question here is: were you ever there under your own free will? Even when you didn't know any better? If you wanted to leave, you couldn't *but* you didn't want to leave. I suppose it's a philosophical question; it conjures all sorts of ideas about the nature of free will and determinism, but I think about this now for another reason. I consider the choices in my life that have led me to this moment and realise they weren't really my choices at all, they were my parents' choices first. After all, they raised me to be the man I am, they supplied the raw materials. And their choices, even before I had taken my first steps, have impacted on my life. It's a reality check when you realise you haven't necessarily had control. I'm not in control of this now, I have never been in control. Everything led me here. I *chose* to come here but I'm beginning to realise that even if I wanted to leave, I would find that the door is locked.

# FIVE

OUR APARTMENT IS probably not quite big enough for a party but last year when Samuel asked if he could have end of year drinks with his friends, I said yes. If I hadn't, he'd probably have asked his father, at his much bigger, much nicer house. In the eyes of his friends, that would have made Marko the *cool* parent and that's the last thing I wanted.

I said yes because I knew with the restrictions it would only be a handful of them, his very closest friends, and it would also mean that I could meet Jessica again. The dinner hadn't gone particularly well, and she didn't seem to be going away anytime soon. I thought I'd try to understand what it was that captivated Samuel so. There must be something beneath the rehearsed decorum and perfectly brushed blonde hair. It was a warm afternoon, and the heat was likely to spill into the night. I bought bags of chips and some beers for Samuel. I had planned out my viewing for the night, a series on Netflix would keep me in my bedroom so I wouldn't interrupt their gathering too much. I told Samuel I'd have my earphones in and a glass of wine in hand. 'The place is yours.'

'Thanks, Mum.'

And that's what I did. I stayed there in my room and I watched the trashy reality TV with the volume high enough to block out the music. In a break between episodes, I turned the sound down a little and heard the conversation grow animated. It was clear that they were a few drinks in by this stage. I paused my show to listen to them.

'It's morally ambiguous at best,' someone said.

'You can't blame anyone for doing it,' the boy with the high-pitched voice, Tyler, contributed.

'I don't think you could say to someone *you can't procreate*.' That was Evan's voice. 'Or would this rule just be for certain people?'

'Would that be a bad thing?' Tyler said.

'What?' the first voice added.

'If you had to, like, pass a test or something before having kids?'

'Of course it's a bad thing,' Samuel said, a hint of laugher in his voice. 'That's the dictionary definition of discrimination. You're dividing the populace and discriminating against one group who you believe to be less intelligent. It's eugenics. I'm not saying you're wrong about overpopulation but that's not the way to fix the problem.'

'It's the religious groups,' someone else interrupted. 'They all have ten kids each. Half of them don't believe in birth control.'

'Well, we can't do what China did, can we? Especially now that designer babies are possible. The Chinese just all wanted boys to carry their family names. Same thing would probably happen around the world, people would want a specific thing if they could only have one.'

I noted uncomfortably that neither of the two women in the room had spoken, yet the boys were speaking with such authority. I doubted the girls' silence was because they had nothing to contribute; I was sure they had strong views themselves. I'd been there when I was younger, stuck listening to Marko and his friends argue, without expecting or inviting input from anyone else. Mind you, back then they were arguing about whether Pearl Jam was a better band than Nirvana.

'Procreation is a biological imperative,' Samuel said. 'You can't just out-think it. Some people need to have kids. People don't think about the bigger picture, just about their own worlds, their own lives. The environment is just this abstract concept to them, not as real as their family.'

I could never be so eloquent or clever but he was saying what I was thinking. You can't always just resist your natural urges. Having a baby gave my life meaning.

'What about for you?' Jessica's voice at last.

The room seemed to inhale.

'Me?'

'Is it a biological imperative for you?'

'Well, I don't know,' Samuel said. 'I haven't given it much thought really.' I could feel the tension in the air, even from under the covers in my bedroom.

'I think we're getting ahead of ourselves here,' Tyler's voice again. 'You've not been together long enough to have that chat.' He laughed but no-one else did. Suddenly, the apartment seemed to heat a few degrees. I cringed, waiting to hear what happened next.

'Vape?' a new voice said, breaking the tension. I was almost grateful for the interruption; maybe that would put the conversation to bed for the night.

'Out on the balcony,' Samuel said. 'I'll keep you company.' The ranch slider scraped open.

'I'll come outside too,' Jessica said, escaping Tyler and the awkwardness.

When the ranch slider to the deck was closed again, they continued speaking. Tyler spoke first. 'God, how annoying is she,' he said, his voice low. '*Is it a biological imperative for you?*' he mimicked her with a laugh. 'She's so needy.'

'I know, but they're pretty smitten,' the other girl said.

'She has got a power over him.' I detected a note of anger in his voice. 'It's not right, she's changing him.'

'You've heard the rumours about her?' It's the girl again.

'What? That she's religious?' This time the voice belongs to Evan.

'Well, I heard this from a friend who grew up in the country with her. A guy in my politics class. Apparently, wherever she's from, somewhere in the country, her dad leads some fundamentalist church.'

Just then, the ranch slider opened and the others came back in. 'What are you guys babbling on about in here? I've had enough talking about politics.'

'Oh,' Tyler said, 'just talking about a professor at uni.'

'Alright, well, move over, I'm getting a pack of cards. We're playing drinking games,' Samuel said. 'Let's just get drunk and celebrate the fact uni is over for the year instead of acting like we're in a lecture hall.'

Tyler spoke next. 'Are you getting drunk too, Jessica?'

I swallowed, rising to move closer to the door to listen in. 'I'll have a glass of wine,' she said. 'Sure.'

'You don't have to—' Samuel began but she interrupted.

'One glass won't hurt.'

And that was it. I found myself siding with Jessica over Tyler's nasty remarks but I was still curious about her response. *One glass won't hurt.* So she really was one of those people who seldom drink.

•

Now I go into his room, the sun is rising outside and my eyes sting from sleeplessness. Moo follows me in, meowing at me to fill her bowl.

'One second,' I say to her. She leaps up on his bed.

He'd shown Jessica photos of himself as a baby, and now I see he's pulled one out of the old photo album and left it beside his bed. It's him in his father's arms at about nine months. Marko is looking up over his head, with a frown at me. I remember it, taking that photo. He didn't like to pose much. He hated photos and in this one in particular I practically had to force him to sit down. The seams were already coming apart, the writing was on the wall. He'd be gone a couple of years after the photo was taken. So what is it about this photo, that scowling expression, that interested Samuel enough to pull it out, and leave it beside his bed? Did he show this to Jessica? *This is my Dad*, did he say? *He's a bit of an asshole.* And maybe she told him about her dad. What if she really was converting my son to her religion? I let out a small laugh. Unlikely. Samuel wouldn't be converted so easily.

*Meow.*

'Alright, alright. Hold your horses.' I stride to the kitchen and dump two days' worth of dry food in Moo's bowl. 'Happy now?' She doesn't respond, just buries her face in her food.

'That's what I thought.'

# SIX

A LITTLE LATER in the morning, I go to the pharmacy – one of the few things still permitted. I fill the prescription for the meds. One a day, that's what it says on the box. I'm supposed to stay on them for a few months. You can't just take them when you're feeling down.

Back home, in the kitchen, I take a pill, throw it back with a glass of water. Now I wait to feel better. I go to my room . . . and see something that nails my feet to the carpet. My heart slams. Moo is on my bed and in her mouth is a bird.

'Moo,' I say, approaching her. 'Stop, you'll kill it.'

Moo leaps off the bed and races by me, her back low. I chase her to the living area, she flies under the couch and turns around so when I drop down onto one knee and peer under, I see her eyes.

'Moo, let it go!' I reach out and her paw meets my hand. A slap, no claws, but I know it's a warning. She normally only gives one before she'll draw blood. I reach out tentatively. She growls. There's only one thing for it. I go to the kitchen, quickly peel a can of tuna open and take it back, letting her see and smell it. Then I dump it in her bowl and she comes running, this time without the bird in her mouth. I might be able to save it I think, running back to the lounge. I reach in under the couch, feel its hard body, wet from being in Moo's mouth. I pull it out and find it stiff.

There's no blood and the body is rigid, the eyes open. It's not a real bird. Or it's not a real *living* bird. It's a taxidermy rainbow lorikeet. With wire around its feet so it can stand upright and black lifeless eyes. But it looks so real, with its head turned and wings tight to its body.

'Where did this come from, Moo?'

It must be Samuel's. I take it back to his room. I must have left his wardrobe open when I had been in here earlier. But where did he get it from?

Moo, now full of tuna and two days' worth of dry food, comes in and wraps herself around my shins, rubbing up gently and purring.

'You played me like a fiddle, didn't you?'

•

Around midday, I head out for my daily permitted exercise. There are no police at the park, although I do see a police car parked up on the road. And two soldiers in military fatigues and face masks stand beside the entrance. Samuel's message still doesn't feel right, and I haven't heard from him since.

It's a crisp spring day and I soon notice someone else on my track. That's not uncommon, but I've not seen her before and she is walking the exact route I take, about 100 metres behind me. She *isn't* running like most people do. She's got black hair, and she wears large dark glasses blocking her eyes just above the black mask that covers her mouth. When I get to the far corner of the park and stop for just a moment to turn back, she is still there, walking quickly behind me. Still 100 or so metres back and those dark glasses are turned in my direction. I keep walking. There's a ball of trepidation in my stomach, but I don't know exactly why.

Now, as I start back around toward the apartment, I see she is a little closer. She's striding to catch up. It's broad daylight, yet the way she heads toward me, my trepidation morphs into something a little darker: fear. I move faster now, searching about for other people. The police are always monitoring this area, making sure everybody is exercising alone, but now I see none. My quick walking stride graduates to a run, and my hand goes to my pocket, reaching for the keys to the building. I turn off the track, find a break in the traffic and shoot across the road. Now over my shoulder, I see her there. The lights change right as she's approaching. Four lanes of cars zoom past between us. I stand, looking at her peering through the traffic. She continues to watch me, then her hand rises slowly as if she's waving but it just stays up in the air. Black hair, fair skin.

It's hard to tell much more about her other than she's thin, with skinny legs in lululemon and a light running top.

Before there is another break in traffic, I dash to the front of the building, turn the key and get inside.

Upstairs inside my apartment, I close the door behind me. By the time I get to the balcony and look down, the woman is gone. Where did this fear come from? Was it just a coincidence? Someone walking the same track as me? But then she seemed to gesture from across the road.

I go through my usual routine, settling in for a Friday night at home. I replace my running shoes with slippers, turn the TV on and go to the pantry for a glass of wine. We all have our habits, the processes we follow when we are on autopilot. I curl up on the couch, Moo comes over and I sip my wine, with my phone close by.

Other than the one message, I've not heard from Samuel again. He doesn't have a job but he gets a student allowance, though it's hardly enough to live on. I want to look after him, and I've ordered enough groceries for two. I could always have meals delivered. Then I remember who he is with, and the way she picked at my spaghetti bolognaise as though there was something off with it. I drink my glass of wine and watch some mind-numbing reality TV. It helps to anaesthetise my brain but still those dark thoughts come. I'm back there in the car. I hear Marko's voice from that night.

'Shit,' he said. 'Shit!' He slammed his hand on the steering wheel. 'What the hell was that?'

I opened my mouth but couldn't speak. Blood was pounding in my ears.

'You hit someone,' I finally said, squeezing the words out. I started to cry. 'Marko, you hit someone. They were on a bike.'

'No,' he said, shaking his head wildly. 'No, it wasn't a person. I think I hit a sign. Or an animal.' He was breathing heavily. He started the car again and began moving forward.

'Marko, we've got to stop. We've got to help them.'

'There was no-one.' The anger in his voice surprised me. 'There was no-one on a bike. I just bumped a sign. That's all. A sign. You didn't see what you think you did.' The booze caused his words to crash into each other.

His nostrils were rapidly flaring; his hands squeezed the wheel so tight the veins popped on his forearms. He dropped me at home then went out again. I was in bed weeping when he got in. I heard him take a shower and finally he came to bed. He didn't say anything, he didn't need to.

'The car is gone,' he said.

'Gone?'

'It's in storage. Where it will stay. We can never talk about it.'

'Is he okay?'

Marko just shook his head. 'I don't know. I'm sure he's fine.' A beat passed. He clamped his hand to his forehead. 'I just don't know.'

The next day we saw the news article. A man in critical condition. A father, with a six-year-old son and a one-year-old daughter.

It was raining when it happened. Marko was drunk, but the cyclist didn't have lights on his bike when he was on the road – which is against the law. I know it's not the same as drink driving, but who is to say that Marko would have hit him if he'd had a red light on his seat pole like he was supposed to? That was Marko's logic, the one time he mentioned it, and for years I bought into it. We all come up with little lies or half-truths we continually tell ourselves to get through the long open hours of the day. Marko was over the limit, but he was in control of the vehicle. Neither of us saw him, not until he was rolling up the bonnet of the car, over the roof, the bike hurtling onto the footpath.

'We never talk about it again,' he said. 'Understand?'

And I did understand. I would mention it to him once again, about a year later, but not since then. Not to anyone. But secrets grind you down over time. I've always tried to instil this idea in Samuel.

By the time I've finished the bottle of wine, I'm halfway through a season of the show. When I get up to make dinner, I find the room lurches. I can barely keep my eyes open too. I recall the medication, the doctor's warning. If you must drink, make sure it's not excessive. *What is excessive?* It feels like that ship has sailed now. I forgot all about the pills.

I get to the kitchen and open the fridge to make dinner, but I don't seem to have the coordination to cook anything too demanding, so microwaved pasta-for-one it is. I feed Moo, bending down to put food in her bowl and when I stand upright, my head spins. Over the hum of the microwave, I hear something from my bedroom. A chiming sound. It's a video call. I move as quickly as my sluggish feet can carry me. The downlights have tails that swirl as my head rocks with each step. I get to my laptop, open on Facebook on my dresser, and see his name: *Samuel*. I quickly flatten my hair with my palms, stretch my eyes wide open and accept the call.

'Hello?' I say to the dark screen. 'Hello, Samuel? Are you there?' Suddenly the screen lights up, and I can see him. He's right there before me, staring into the camera with those dark eyes. His scraggy hair hangs down around his face and he has a little stubble now, in patches on his chin and around his jawline. I realise in that moment that he wouldn't have his razor or toothbrush; I could send them to him.

'Hello? Can you hear me, Samuel?' He frowns now and seems to be focusing on something else on the screen. The image is pixelated but I know it's him. When he speaks, the sound is slightly out of sync with his mouth.

'Mum, hi,' he says, a grin. It's real, top teeth showing, laughter lines appearing around his eyes. He's happy to see me; he hasn't just left me behind.

'Samuel,' I say. 'Finally. God, I've been trying to get onto you for the past two days. I was so worried.'

'I know,' he says. Behind him is a cement block wall, some shelves with books I can't make out. A picture of a horse mid-stride. Above him is a cream-coloured ceiling and a naked bulb. 'I'm so sorry, Mum, I only just got your messages. I left my phone charger at home, so my phone has been flat. I only charged it this morning. And now the internet is scratchy here.'

'Why don't you call me on the phone then?'

'No,' he says. 'I wanted to see your face.'

I feel something thawing inside. He's a sweet boy. 'Where are you?'

'I'm just at Jessica's. I know it's not ideal but when my battery was flat and we were out, I just decided it might be easier. I know I got in your hair a little last time and it could be good to have some time apart, right?' An open expression, eyebrows slightly raised above the bridge of his nose.

'In my hair? No, not at all. I thought we did okay. I enjoyed spending time together.'

'Well, I didn't know that. I'm sure you wouldn't last another six weeks with me if this lockdown gets extended like the last one.'

*Of course, I would,* I think, but I say, 'Yeah, that's probably right. I'm sure it's for the best. So what is the actual address?'

He smiles. 'I'll have to get it for you and send it through; I'm not entirely certain but I'll grab it tonight.'

'Right, okay. But just the street?'

He scratches the back of his neck. The picture refreshes so slowly that I see his hand at the top of his neck then the bottom, then he's touching his chin.

'I'm not sure, Mum. I'll send it through when I can.'

'You can't just ask Jessica?'

'No. I'll send it to you soon. She's busy.'

'Please do. I want to post you a care package; your toothbrush and razor are here, and I can send you some treats. Are you within five kilometres of home? Maybe we can cross paths when we are walking or at the supermarket?'

'Ah, I don't think so,' he says, and my heart sinks. I really won't see him properly in the flesh until this is all over. 'But we can chat a lot and have lots of video calls.'

I still feel dazed. Jessica said she lived in a new apartment in the city so am I seeing this right? The bricks behind him, the pictures and that ring of water damage on the ceiling – it all looks old. It doesn't look like a modern apartment at all but a sort of dungeon. 'What's her place like?'

'It's nice.' He looks around him. 'Don't let this room fool you, it's actually quite a cool place. This is just the office-slash-study so it's a bit gross in here. But this is where the reception for the internet is best.'

'And where is she, Jessica?'

'Oh, she's in the other room.' He smiles again. I sense he's not telling me the full story. 'So what have you been up to?'

'Not much really. Went to the pharmacy, took a walk around the park.' I don't tell him about the wine, the antidepressants. The argument with his father.

'Nice,' he says. I lean in closer; it still feels like my eyes are deceiving me because I could swear that's a basement he's in, but I know the cocktail of $8 merlot and SSRI medication probably isn't helping my powers of perception.

'Well, I've got to run – we're having dinner soon.'

'Oh sure, I've got something cooking too.'

'Good timing then. Let's talk again in the next couple of days.'

'Of course,' I say. 'Call me whenever you want to chat, okay? Please take care and make sure you also message me if you need anything sent over, or money or anything.'

He's got that big happy smile again. 'Okay, Mum. I think I'll be alright. I've got clothes and he's looking after me here.'

I swallow, but something seems to lodge in my throat. I stare at him, still looking back at me. 'Wait, did you say just say *he?*' *Isn't it just Jessica,* I think. *Did I hear right? What could he mean by* he's *looking after me here?*

There's a delay again. His face is frozen and the sound cuts out.

'Son? Are you there?'

His face is contorted, mid-speech, frozen like that. Then the screen goes black. He's gone. The call drops out. *How did you rate the quality of that call?* the screen asks me. I click one star. Then I call him back. I find I'm swaying where I sit on my bed and the room is turning a little. The call doesn't get through. I see he is offline. Maybe the sound froze for a second, cutting off the *s* sound from 'she's'. But why didn't Jessica say hello?

My lips feel numb while I eat the now lukewarm pasta. On the couch with the TV on, I analyse the conversation. It was odd, there's no other way of putting it. Samuel seemed off, the room didn't fit in with the apartment Jessica supposedly lives in and he seemed to avoid certain areas of the conversation. *He's.* That was the word that has jagged in my brain like a fishhook. *He's*. Who is *he* when it was supposed to be her, *she*, Jessica?

Moo leaps up at the other end of the couch, and curls in on herself.

The room is still oscillating a little. I take my phone and call Marko. It rings for a long time before he answers.

'I spoke to him,' I say.

'Good. So he's safe? We can move on then.'

'He seemed off. I don't know. The video was a little out of sync with the sound and he was in, like, a basement or something.'

'Are you okay?'

'What?'

'Your voice is slurred; you don't sound very lucid at all.'

'I'm fine, Marko,' I say, the words clumsily tumbling out. 'I'm fine.'

'Jesus, Lou. You called him like this, he's probably the one who is worried. Pull your head in.'

'He said *he's*.'

'Sorry?'

'He said *he*, not she. Who is *he*?'

Marko doesn't speak, I can hear a rasping sound like he's running his palm over stubble near the phone. 'It's Lou again,' I hear him say to someone, probably *her*. 'She's out of it. I don't know.'

'I can hear you,' I say. 'It's not what you think. I'm not out of it.' I sigh. I won't mention the medication. It won't help matters.

'*He's*? That's what you're calling about. A word that really means nothing, a word you probably misheard because you're wasted. I honestly don't know what is going through your mind. Do you need attention, is that it? Are you so lonely there that you have to call your son and ex-husband just so you have something to do?'

'No,' I say, the shock of his words sobering me a little. 'Of course not, how can you say that?'

'Because you have no evidence that anything is wrong. In fact, you have evidence to the contrary. Everything is fine. Your son is safe.'

*Your,* I note. Not *our* son. 'He's still your son, despite how much you try to scrub us from your life.'

'Anything else, Lou?'

'Someone followed me in the park.' It just comes out. I wish the words were physical things floating in the air before me. Something I could grab and shove back into my mouth before Marko notices, but it's too late. He heard it and it's only now that I realise how unhinged I sound.

'Someone is following *you* now, are they?' he says it loudly, and I realise it's for the benefit of *her*. He's mocking me. I can imagine him twirling a finger next to his temple to signal my cognitive decline. 'So interesting, Lou. Do you think it might be the federal police, or maybe it's that cult from out in the bush, come to snatch you away, like they did those children? Do you think it could be that?'

'It's not funny. Don't mock me.'

'I know it's not funny, but I don't really have time for this. You need to lay off the booze for a bit.'

'They followed me all the way to my building. I'm not making it up. I don't know who or why. What if they were scoping out the place?' I feel hysterical. I try to rein it in, but it keeps coming. 'I'm telling you, something isn't right. Samuel is in a city apartment, so how could the internet be so bad that it freezes and crashes?'

'Ever heard of the National Broadband Network? It's been a disaster; I can barely watch a movie without it buffering.'

'Someone has done something to him.'

'No, Lou, you've done something to him. You've scared him off. He's left home to hunker down with someone else and now you're having a breakdown because you're realising he's the only thing you had and that now you've ruined it.'

'Marko!' I hear his new wife down the line, admonishing him. 'That's enough.'

'No, you're right. I am a waste of space,' I tell him. 'I'm everything you told me I was for all those years. I wasn't back then, but eventually I believed it. You did this, Marko. And if I'm right, if something has happened, it will be your fault for not believing me. Then you'll have to live with it.'

'I think I'll survive. You, on the other hand, will likely need a good stint in a psychiatric ward.'

'You think you'd survive if something happened to our son? Is that what you just said?'

'No,' he says, as if offended. 'Of course not. You're delusional. Don't start putting words in my mouth.'

'You're sociopathic.'

'I'm hanging up. Sober up, take a long hard look in the mirror, Lou. It's getting embarrassing.'

I drop the phone on the couch, waking Moo who leaps, on four paws, back arched. He's not the man I married. Either that or he has always concealed his true nature. We've been apart for a decade and a half, but he's never been this mean before. I tip my head back over the edge of the couch so I'm staring up at the ceiling and stay like that, thinking about that one single word. *He's. He's. He's.* I know that woman at the park is part of this. *He's.* It throbs in my ears like a heartbeat. I send Marko a message; I know I shouldn't but I'm still trembling with anger. *Maybe I am an alcoholic mess, and maybe I'll get too drunk and accidentally spill the beans on our little secret.* It takes me longer than it should to type the words out, my thumbs keep hitting the wrong letters. *Our* secret. Not just *his.* We're both in this but he's in it deeper. I see three dots appear: he's typing a message, then they're gone again.

It's after eight now, so no-one at all is out on the street or in the park. Everything is closed. I have nothing to worry about, but still I feel the itch of fear. I hear sounds in the night. A door of another unit in the building slams. Someone's TV is up too loud. I manage to peel myself off the couch and drag myself to my bed where I collapse into a dark pool of sleep.

●

When I wake, too early, always too early, it's with a dry throat and a monster of a hangover that squeezes my brain in its talons and twists my vision so slowly that the room seems to contort. I dip my head under the kitchen faucet and suck in a mouthful of water like a dog. The water tastes almost sweet, I gulp it down in hungrily. Hangovers don't normally feel this bad. Before long, I'm at the toilet folded over the bowl and last night's partially digested pasta sprays from me, along with the water I've just swallowed. The vomiting helps clear the nausea, but I still feel fatigued and the headache is getting worse. Note to self: never combine your new meds with a bottle of wine. *How am I going to get through this?*

I get to the couch and place a bowl on the floor beside me. I need help. Maybe a visitor would be nice, someone to nurse me back to health. I personally know three people who broke the rules the last lockdown. Not in an *Oops, I stood within 1.5 metres of a stranger* way but more a *I'm going to go have sex with a stranger I met on the internet* way. That was Zara, one of my girlfriends. Another was Vikki's husband who drove two hours into the country to see his sick mum, breaking about four different lockdown restrictions and risking thousands in fines. The third, I'm ashamed to say, was Samuel.

At the time, he and Jessica were spending so much of their time on video calls, talking every day, deep into the night. They were intimate partners, so they could see each other so long as they weren't out after curfew. Then at about the three-week mark, he disappeared in the night. I don't know when he left, I just know that when I woke, he wasn't there. And he didn't get back in until lunch.

He came home with his tail between his legs.

'Where were you?' I asked before he'd even closed the door of the apartment.

'I went to see Jessica.'

'Well, you can do that, I guess. But why didn't you tell me? Why did you go in the middle of the night?'

'I know I should have told you. It was, um . . . something important.'

'Alright, well, next time don't break curfew and make sure you let me know,' I said.

When I asked him what was so important that he had to leave in the middle of the night, he was evasive.

'Oh,' he said, his gaze meeting mine only for a second before sliding away. 'Um, well, it was just some family drama she was having.'

'Sounds like the girl who cried wolf,' I said. 'So, go on, tell me. What was the family drama?'

He drew a breath. 'I don't want to go through it all right now.' His chin fell and he scratched at his jaw. 'She was just upset, that's all. Her family is religious. She needed me.'

There was something Samuel wasn't telling me. I watched his face, which at that point remained fixed on the phone in his hands as he punched away at a text message. I'd always, *always*, taught him to do the right thing, to be honest. I'd raised him to see the toxic nature of secrets and yet here he was with something he wasn't telling me and I could see it pained him.

And then there was another suspicious conversation, just a week or so ago. Again, as I put the pieces together, it seems maybe he was trying to tell me something. Maybe he'd promised someone else he would keep it a secret and he didn't want to break that promise, while also wanting to bring me in.

'How hard is it to adopt?'

'Adopt?'

'Can anyone just adopt a kid or is there, like, screening?'

'Sorry?'

'Like if someone put a baby up for adoption, who could take the baby in?'

'Um, well, couples who apply, I suppose.'

He looked concerned, serious. He'd been in a mood. I can't remember exactly what had brought it about, but this was the first conversation we had after he snapped out of it.

'Well, I mean, take you and Dad as an example. Say you couldn't have had me. Would you have adopted?'

'Well, now that you mention it, we thought about adopting; it took years for me to fall pregnant,' I say. 'I think we would have qualified, but they definitely have a lot of checks and safeguards to make sure babies end up in supporting and loving environments.'

'What do you mean?'

'I mean, to adopt a baby there are a lot of hoops you have to jump through, and it takes a long time. You don't just turn up and pick a child to take home. It's not easy, most people spend years going through the process. So to answer your question, we would have.'

'Right, so to adopt you need to show you're normal, happy, not like unstable or whatever?'

I'd looked at him long and hard until his gaze shifted away toward the window. 'I guess so,' I'd said. 'Are you thinking about adopting, Samuel?' I'd tried to make a joke of it, but he'd just looked sad.

'No,' he said, as if it wasn't a joke, as if it took serious consideration. 'No, I'm just trying to understand. That's all. I guess it's better when a kid ends up with happy, normal parents than stuck with ones who aren't ready or don't have it in them.'

It seemed odd at that time, but now as I make my way back to my bedroom with the bowl, it seems even stranger. It's still dark out, it must be five in the morning.

Back in bed, I reach for my phone to check the time. I see something that makes me stop dead still, like a bug hit with bug spray. Something I wasn't expecting at all. Missed calls. Why did my son call me in the middle of the night? Would I have woken to answer if I hadn't been so out of it? Moo comes into my room again, that damn taxidermy lorikeet in her mouth. But I guess she can play with it. It doesn't hurt. I watch her pin it between her paws and drag mouthfuls of feathers away as I call his number back. It goes straight to voicemail. I hang up.

*What are you not telling me, Samuel? What is it?*

# SEVEN

REID IS AN acquaintance. For a brief period, he was seeing Viv's brother, Perry. Reid seems like the type of guy who doesn't really have friends. He doesn't want friends, but people are probably fond of him. He's American, in his thirties, and dresses and acts exactly like a man who is trying to disappear in a crowd. Which makes sense, given his job.

Viv gave me his contact details. Reid was a cop in the US years ago, but now in Australia, he's a private investigator. He helped another friend of ours to get favourable terms in a divorce. He turned up old records from a brothel in Sarah's ex's bank statement. The payment had come through as a purchase from a bookstore in South Melbourne.

'Should have known myself actually,' Sarah had told me. 'Who spends three hundred dollars at a bookstore at ten pm on a Tuesday?'

I'm thinking of recruiting Reid to help me. That odd video call last night did nothing to ease my concerns. Then the missed late-night calls at around two this morning stirred an anxious feeling inside that continues to grow and grow. Nothing is worse than a hangover when you've got something like this on your mind. It's normally post-drinking regret, *What did I do, what did I say last night when I was drunk?* But this time it's worse. *What did I miss? What could I have done to help my son?*

I make my coffee as black as oil seep and drink two cups of it. I'm re-energised or reanimated at least. Then I make a bowl of muesli and take it to the couch where I call Reid on speaker phone. It's a good sign that he answers; he can't be on a job.

'Reid,' he says, by way of greeting.

'Hi, it's Lou here, I'm friends with Viv . . . and, ah, Perry.' He doesn't speak, so I add, 'You helped out my friend Sarah with her divorce, we've met briefly before.'

'Oh, right,' he says. 'Yeah, that rings a bell. Lou, was it?'

'Yes, that's right. I'm calling to see if you can help me with something.'

I still have redundancy money coming in. It was a good package in the end. It included sessions with a therapist, my sick leave and holiday leave paid out in full. We have a good union. *Had.* I don't have a union at all anymore.

'What are you looking for exactly, Lou? Hard to do too much in this city while it's all locked down.'

'Well, can you do work remotely?'

'I can, I do. I can also get out and about if need be. What is it?'

'It's a long story.'

'I've got time.'

'It's my son, he's gone AWOL.' He doesn't speak, and I think of ways to fill the silence. 'He's not one to disappear, a good kid.'

'When you say disappeared . . .'

'He says he's at his girlfriend's place. But I didn't hear from him for twenty-four hours before he finally got in touch.'

'But he did get in touch?'

'He did, but he video-called me from his laptop. And that's the thing. He seems off. Like he doesn't want to be where he is.'

'Under duress?'

I think about it. 'Possibly. Yes. I think he could be. And then he rang me in the middle of the night, from his phone a few times, but I was asleep.'

'How old?'

'Nineteen.'

'And this isn't normal for him? A nineteen-year-old kid wanting to be with his girlfriend?'

'No. He's acting totally out of character. Something was off with him.' *Although with the meds and the booze, something was off with me too.*

'What do you mean?'

'Well, the video call wasn't good and he seemed almost like he was acting, or hiding something, I don't know. She's supposed to live in this apartment building in the city but it looked like a basement behind him.'

'Okay, okay. I'm sure it's nothing but you want peace of mind, right?'

'Yeah.'

He pauses for a moment. 'Look, I'll help if I can. I'll do it for ninety-five an hour plus expenses, but I doubt I'll have any. I'm not likely to be staking out any locations, and it will mostly be online. It won't take too long to get to the bottom of it.'

I think about the price, doing the maths in my head, but I know I don't have a choice. I need help. 'Thank you, Reid. That's fine.'

'You've not spoken to the girlfriend or seen her?'

'No, she wasn't in the room on the video call.'

'Have you ever been to her place, dropped your son off there, anything like that?'

'No.'

'And I take it you don't have an address for her?'

'No, but my son rides his bike there sometimes or even walks, so it can't be too far. But then he implied it wasn't within five kilometres. He doesn't lie to me.'

'He's a teenaged boy, and he doesn't lie to his mother?'

'That's right,' I insist. 'He's honest. He always has been. No secrets, that was our rule. But I could tell when we spoke that something was off – he was different, he was keeping something from me.'

'Okay. I'll give you my email. Have you got a pen?'

'Yeah.'

He dictates an email address to me, which I scribble down, my hand shaking.

'What I need from you is: your son's full name, date of birth, hair colour, eye colour, any photos you might have. I need his phone number along with the girlfriend's details, any other pertinent information you have about her. How long they've been together. Where did they meet. Social media profiles, that sort of thing.'

'All their social media?'

'Yes, plus anything obscure outside of the usual suspects. Any Chan websites, Reddit, message boards or forums, Twitch. Anything you think that could be important that I wouldn't find on a cursory search. The less I have to dig myself, the less time I spend and the less I will charge you.'

'Okay, I'll send it all through to you today.'

'Just run me through the timeline once more. When was the last time you saw him in the flesh?'

'Nine am on Wednesday.'

'And you saw him on a video call last night?'

'Yes.'

'What service?'

'Sorry?'

'Skype, Zoom, Facebook Messenger?'

'Oh, ah, Facebook Messenger.'

'What time was that?'

'Eight pm last night. The call just randomly cut out. There was another thing. He's supposed to be at her apartment, but he said, "*He's* taking good care of me", when he should have said, "*She's* taking good care of me."'

'Okay. That could be something but let's not jump to conclusions.'

'He was supposed to visit his father after lunch, but he didn't. That's not completely uncommon; sometimes he stays on later at the library or forgets stuff like that.'

'Right. I'd like you to send me your husband's details too.'

'Will you contact him?'

'Would that be a problem?'

I consider it. 'Um, yeah, it would actually. He thinks I'm being melodramatic.'

'If you'd prefer, I won't get in contact with him, but if you give me an address, I can drive by and try to check if your son is there, just to eliminate that as an avenue. What's the desired outcome? Just check his safety?'

'I want him home,' I say, knowing it's the truth but hating myself for it. I've become a needy mum. Maybe Marko is right; he knows that Samuel is all I have. That's why he's not so panicked about all of this. 'First priority is obviously to check in on him, but I do want him to come back so I can look after him. I don't trust this girl, never have. She's religious, not that I have a problem with that, but she's just off.'

'I'll do a background check, see if I can dig anything up. I have contacts that can get information that's not available to the public.'

'Thank you, it's such a relief having someone who knows what they're doing helping me. I feel like I've been going crazy.'

'Well, I'll look forward to receiving your email and I'll call you back when I have any news, and likewise contact me with any updates at your end. For now, look after yourself. Oh, one last thing. I'll send you through some software to record your calls. Install it on your phone and computer and whenever you hear from him, start the software and if there's anything important, please send me the recordings.'

'Is that legal?'

'That's my least favourite question,' he says. 'In the state of Victoria, it is legal to record private conversations unless you're representing a business. But there are certain things you cannot do with that recording.'

'Right.'

'Speak again soon,' he says. Then he's gone.

I open my laptop and start typing out the email, filling in as many details as I can. I add in a couple of notes about Samuel's relationship with Jessica. If nothing is off, if everything is as it seems, this will all seem like the obsession of some borderline-alcoholic, overbearing cow trying to control her son, but that's a risk I'm willing to take – because if there is a one-in-a-million chance that my suspicions are right and I do nothing about it, I could regret it for the rest of my life. This is what all those years at customs prepared me for, moments like this when I can only rely on my judgement and gut feel. When I've typed the email up, I review it all, find it covers the bases well enough. Reid shoots back a reply almost immediately.

*Excellent. This is a good start, lots to work with. See the file attached. Open it on your phone and laptop to access the download.*

The file is named *VidSafe Call Recorder*. I double-click it and a download box pops up. When it's installed, I check to make sure it's working. I open Facebook and video-call Samuel again. This time, he answers almost straightaway.

The picture is much clearer now, the reception improved from last time. I can see him, my son. I feel relief that he's there, safe and sound. The room doesn't have any natural light, just that single bulb hanging above his head, but still, it's enough to see the shape of him, his features. Those big brown eyes and the scruffy hair. The patchy stubble.

'Hello,' I say. 'Our call ended so quickly last night, I wanted to speak again today.'

'Hi, Mum. Yeah, sorry about that. The line dropped out. Like I said, it's pretty dodgy here.'

'That's what I was calling about actually, did you figure out where "here" is exactly?'

'No, sorry, I forgot to ask, but I'll check soon. It's something like Old Station Street. I don't know.'

'Right,' I say. It doesn't ring a single bell.

'Anyway, what's happening at home?'

'Same old. Pretty boring really. I'll head out for my walk soon.' *But I haven't been out since that woman followed me,* I think. 'Spoke with your father. He probably thinks I'm nuts because I was so worried about you.'

'Oh, Mum. Please don't worry. I'm fine. I feel really bad for not telling you what I was doing. It happened so quickly. One minute, I was at a cafe, the next they were locking the state down and I had to suddenly decide if I could get home in time or if I should lockdown here instead.'

'Yeah, you were a right brat about it, Samuel, but I forgive you.'

'How's Moo?'

'She's good,' I say. I don't mention his bird that she destroyed. He can find out about that later. 'She's doing my head in trying to catch flies against the window, though.'

He smiles at that. It's good to see him with a grin. The bricks behind him make it look almost like a prison. I try to tell myself that it's just what new apartment buildings look like.

'Could you show me around the place, Samuel? Take the laptop for a walk?'

He looks uncertain. 'No, I wish I could but there's no wi-fi so I'm hard-wired to the wall, I'm afraid.'

*He'd told me there was wi-fi before. He said the wi-fi was sketchy. He's lying.* He would never lie; only if telling the truth would put him in some sort of danger. That's just who he is: always doing the right thing. I feel that stone of trepidation in my chest again. 'Maybe turn the laptop so I can see the room.'

'Ahh, sure okay,' he says. He does. He quickly swings the laptop clumsily one way, then the other. In one corner, I see filing cabinets. In another, I see a camp bed set up in the corner.

'Was that a bed?'

'Oh, yeah, that. It's just a spare, I think.'

*For what other people? We are in lockdown.* 'Samuel,' I say. 'Is there something you're not telling me?'

His cheeks glow. 'Like what?'

'Well, why did you call me back last night at two am?'

'Oh, I didn't realise how late it was. The internet had cut out so, when I went to bed, I thought I'd try you on your phone.'

'Bed at two?'

'Yeah, we were playing cards. Lost track of time.'

'Okay, why haven't I seen Jessica then?'

He looks perplexed. 'You want to see Jessica?'

'I do.'

He sits for a moment thinking. 'Um, okay, give me a second. I'll see if she's free.'

He angles the laptop screen down so I can't see the door, just the keyboard and the edge of the wooden desk. I hear footsteps getting quieter. Then he comes back. The camera tilts up. 'Sorry, Mum, she's a bit tied up.'

There's a whine in the background; it's a power tool or . . . something else, maybe an infant, I think. The sound quality makes it hard to tell.

'One sec,' he says now, standing to slam the door closed. The sound disappears.

'Mum, I'll call you back okay?' he says. 'I've got to run.'

'What was that?' I say. 'Was that a baby?' But before I can say another word, the call ends.

*How would you rate this call?* pops up. I close it. Then something else pops up: *Would you like to save recording?* The recording software worked. After saving the file, I find it on my desktop and drag it into an email to Reid. Then I watch it back. I slow it right down at the moment there was that sound. It's a high-pitched howl. But now I find myself second-guessing it. Could it be a scream from a horror movie on too loud in the other room? Could it be the neighbours? But it's not just the sound. It's the look, the wide eyes, the question on Samuel's face and the sudden departure. If I saw a look like that at customs, I'd be sending him through for an interview. It's a guilty look. My fear for my son is morphing into something else now. A deeper suspicion about the entire situation. Come to think of it, it's been months since I saw Jessica. What if that was a baby? What if that was *his* baby? It's possible, I realise now, that I'm a grandmother and my son is hiding it from me. But why?

# EIGHT

IT'S ALL FALLING into place. That's why he needed to be there so badly. Maybe he's not in trouble, he's just . . . gone and had a baby. A baby with her. So why are they hiding out together? Two people in their late teens should be sharing this news with their friends and family and letting us help and support them. *What if the truth doesn't set you free? What if the truth is the cage?* That's what his YouTube account said, and his response made it clear it's about family, but what if he meant him and Jessica? What if *daddy issues* was about him becoming a father? Now he's cooped up with her in that apartment with a screaming baby and no support, it can't be easy. I feel sick now thinking about it. All his questions about adoption and who might adopt a child make sense. They might have been planning to give it up, because with Jessica's religious background I can see why they wouldn't opt for an abortion.

I wish I could go there and see him, to meet my grandchild, to hold them. It's almost a painful sensation. I imagine their precious little face, the tiny fingers and toes. I think of Samuel as a baby; for those first few months, he would scream and scream. I wouldn't take him anywhere. He was inconsolable. The only thing I could do was feed him; my nipples were constantly cracked and painful. It was hell but it got better eventually. By the time he was a toddler, he was calmer, he could sleep in his own room without being attached to me.

The phone rings, breaking my daydream. It's Reid. I take it out on the balcony and press a cigarette between my lips, lighting it as I answer. I inhale and let the cloud of smoke out as I speak.

'Reid, hi.'

'I've got news. A couple of interesting bits from my preliminaries.'

'I've got news too, but you go first,' I say, then draw on the cigarette again, feel the satisfying flow of smoke into my lungs.

'The girl is from a town called Smith's Rest. Her father is the local minister up there.'

'I knew that he was a minister and I don't care if someone is religious so long as they're not shoving it down my throat,' I say. 'But this adds to a theory I have.'

'Well, we'll get to that. You know, once upon a time this work was just about stake-outs, following people, calling on resources for information; now it's much more about looking into people's online lives. Everyone gives it all up online. You buy a house and post a selfie in front of the sales board and suddenly the world has your new address. You check in at the gym and everyone knows where you work out. You post a run on your exercise app and now I can see where and when you go running. Not to mention Facebook and Twitter which give me insights into how you think, who you associate with. Remember the murder that happened in a holiday rental? With all the cameras? If you can find someone's profile on Airbnb or WeStay, you can see where they holiday. The list goes on. Almost no-one on this planet can avoid leaving a significant trace of their lives and their day-to-day activities online.'

'So what are you saying?'

'I'm saying Jessica is squeaky clean. Or as clean as you can be. There is practically no trace of her other than her very private Facebook which is locked down. No LinkedIn, Twitter, Instagram, Pinterest, TikTok. Whatever. No nothing.'

'Does that mean she's hiding something?'

'Not necessarily. But it says a lot about her. Maybe she just doesn't crave attention, or isn't used to it. Maybe she doesn't need the distraction of social media with her studies. Maybe—'

'She's in hiding.'

'I guess that's possible too. Anyway, I searched for other kids she went to school with, to try to find information on her that way. I found one or two photos of her on other people's social media profiles. Images from a church group.'

'I knew there was something off about that girl. I just knew it.' I draw the last of the cigarette into my lungs, stab it out in the ashtray. 'From the moment I met her.'

'Her father is quite extreme in his Christian views. I would say he's definitely a fundamentalist. Takes things in the Bible quite literally. Her father is Tim J. Yule.'

I think about the name but nothing comes up. 'I'm sorry, who?'

'He's the head of the Breakthrough Church? Look them up.'

'Right,' I say. 'Anything I should be worried about?'

'Well, I think it's worth looking further into it, if we can't track him down through Jessica or your ex.' He exhales. 'Anyway, as far as Jessica goes, I do have an address and I'm waiting to hear back from a contact for a phone number, but she hasn't made it easy for me.'

I feel a rush of excitement. 'How?'

'I have my ways.' He clears his throat. 'Suffice to say it's not always entirely legal what I do.'

A prickle of anxious energy slides in beneath my chest. 'You have her home address? Her apartment?'

'I'll email it through. I saw the recording too. How often do you stay somewhere without at least knowing the street, or what it's near?'

'Never.'

'He's keeping it from you. Where he is. I'm sure of it.'

'And I think I know why . . . I think he might have become a father. He doesn't want me or anyone else finding him.'

A long pause. 'He wouldn't tell you? That's a big thing to keep from your mother.'

I think about the nasal swab packaging I found in his room: what if it wasn't a rapid test, what if he had been testing for something else, something to do with the baby?

'I haven't seen *her* for a while. I might be off the mark here, but I thought I heard a baby in the background last time. A baby screaming out. Maybe they've organised a private adoption.'

He makes a noise in his throat. 'You know your son better than I do, so only you can say if he's capable of that. But if she gave birth at a hospital, it would be registered. Plus the sound could be anything, I thought it was a drill. Something like that.'

'Then he ended the call without much more than a few words.' I sigh. 'I just wish he would tell me what's going on. I want to help.'

'Before the lockdown, you know, over the past few weeks, was he different at all?'

I think about it. I didn't notice too much off but, then again, I wasn't looking for any signs. 'He was out more, and grumpy a lot. Last time we were in lockdown, he went around there in the middle of the night. He's been online more than usual, but it was for an assignment at university. He's taking anthropology, it's all over my head. And yeah, I guess he has been a bit moody. I noticed that.'

'Let me do a little more digging, see what else I turn up, and I'll get in touch in the next couple of days.'

'Thanks, Reid.'

'Don't mention it.'

•

I've not done any exercise since that woman followed me in the park, and now as I take the steps down toward the front door, I'm filled head to toes with butterflies. What if she's out there again?

I put my headphones in and take my phone. As I step outside, I call Marko.

'Lou. More conspiracy theories, I assume?'

'Not funny, Marko.'

He sighs, his breath coming down the line. 'I'm working – can I help you with something?'

'I don't know if you can. Look, I think I should tell you that I'm beginning to suspect that Samuel has a kid.'

A big, deep laugh rattles down the line. 'Pretty certain, are you?'

'It's not really a laughing matter. You could be a grandfather.'

'Does Samuel strike you as the type to keep that from us? Do you really think this is possible, seriously? He's an honest kid.'

'I don't know. Maybe he has a good reason to keep it a secret.'

I'm on the track around the park now. No sign of that woman, thankfully.

Again, that laugh. 'You must be desperately bored in that apartment, Lou. Letting your imagination run wild.'

'You must be desperately selfish to think there's nothing wrong.'

'No, I'm just not deluded,' he fires back. 'You've watched too many soaps. You're projecting your fantasies onto the world around you.'

I ignore him and push on. 'Have you heard from him? Have you tried his phone? It's not working, is it?'

'It's been a couple of days for god's sake. He's in the city with his girlfriend. Probably having lots of sex and enjoying his time with her.'

I feel heat under my arms, not from the walk but from the anger. 'Call him. See for yourself.'

'I will, I have. It didn't get through.'

'Video-call him then. See his face and see the room he's in. That's all I'm asking.'

'Alright, alright. Calm down. I will. I'll speak to him today.'

I draw a breath, hold it in for a second. 'He's our son. *We* are his parents. You don't need to be so hostile and rude.'

It's taken all the courage I have to push these words out and now I wait for his response. It comes eventually.

'Sure, okay, sorry.' I can't tell if he's being sarcastic or not. He lets a few moments pass before he continues. 'This *thing* you have with Jessica is not healthy. I really don't have time for it.'

'There's one other thing,' I say, ignoring his comment. 'Could Samuel have found out about the, um . . .' I can't say it.

I hoped he'd figure out where I was going but he just says, 'The what, Lou? Spit it out.'

'About what happened,' I say, feeling like I'm drowning very slowly. I look around me in the park. No-one is nearby. 'You know. In the past.'

Silence. It stretches on. I count to ten in my head, my entire body tense.

'Oh, come on, this isn't being recorded,' I say, then I realise it probably is. Reid's call recorder is on my phone too.

'We made a promise, Lou. We *both* go down, remember?'

'I know,' I say, through gritted teeth. 'I'm just asking if Samuel might have found out.'

'Not from me,' he says. 'He'd have to be a pretty clever kid to solve a crime from almost two decades ago without any clues.'

'So there's no way?'

'No, I'm careful. Trust me.'

'Okay. I'm careful too. But I'm just checking because he put something on social media. Something about daddy issues. That's all.'

'You mentioning, you know, what happened in the past with us – even just alluding to it. That's what makes me angry. You promised, we had a deal. Never bring it up, do you understand, Lou? Bring it up again and things could get bad between us.'

It sounds like a threat.

'I'm trying to protect *you* more than me, Marko. Can't you see that?'

'Well, that's not exactly true. We were both there and you know as well as I do we both have everything to lose. So, Lou, *never* mention it again. Do you understand? We've made a life after what happened, somehow. I'm not about to let you throw it all away. You can do whatever you want with your second chance. But I am *not* going to let you ruin mine.'

# NINE

BACK HOME, I FLOP onto the couch and put my head in my hands. Marko is right. I've learnt to block out the secret. Even when I think about it, I don't think in concrete terms about what we actually did. I just keep it in a box in my mind that I never open. We are both implicated: we've both kept it quiet all this time and we would both go down. It only works if we each keep our end of the bargain. It's just amazing what you can convince yourself is right. Those things we do, or have done, that are objectively morally wrong, but we manage to block them out and go on with life. That's why I never wanted Samuel to live with secrets. That's probably the scariest part of all of this. Sure, the idea of prison terrifies me, but most of all I fear Samuel knowing: what would he think of his parents then? And what would other people think of me?

None of my lame rationalising or excuses would be of much use if it came out but still that's what my mind does now. I was already at a low point back then, thinking I'd never have a family, but it would have been so much worse if I'd reported what happened when Marko hit the cyclist. So I blocked it out. It's much easier than you would think. And, given the circumstances, it's not as bad as a premeditated crime. We had to go on living, so we did.

I reach for my cigarettes and go out to the balcony but stop myself before I can get one out. I toss the pack into the living room from the balcony, draw a breath of fresh air and look out over the park. I take my phone and scroll Instagram again, just for something to do. I have 210 followers. I know almost all of them, and then there is Bluerazoo11 who for some inexplicable reason has gone through and liked all the photos in my Instagram with Samuel in them. There aren't many. Alarm bells sound inside. I click Bluerazoo11's profile again and see those farm photos, those odd photos of animals. Only now I see they have posted a new one. It's an image of dark curls of hair on dirt. The caption reads *Fresh cut*. I'm keep scrolling, feeling the squeeze of anxious tension in my chest. Something causes a shiver to spread over my skin. The lorikeet. We have a taxidermy lorikeet in this house, and Bluerazoo11 has photos of taxidermy animals on their account. What if they planted it in the apartment?

I swallow hard. It could be anyone. It could be one of Samuel's friends. I have a new idea, remembering what Reid mentioned about Jessica's father. I log out of Instagram and try some searching of my own. Reid was right, there's almost nothing on Jessica but it's not difficult to find Pastor Tim J. Yule, her father. He's got his own newsletter and there are pieces about his church and the effect he's had on the small town. I click a few articles to read up on him. They paint a bleak picture. Church members believe those who have sex before marriage must be punished. They believe abortions should also be punished. Their belief system seems archaic at best.

Then I find an article written by a former member of the church for a literary magazine. I'm prompted by a paywall to subscribe and in my desperation to read it, I enter my credit card details without a second thought. I open and read it with growing dread.

### I Escaped 'Breakthrough', the Smith's Rest Fundamentalist Church

*Two hours northwest of Melbourne, there's a small settlement called Smith's Rest. From 1860 to around 1890, miners descended upon the town, panning the local river for gold. The population swelled, reaching around 10,000 at the peak of the gold rush. Now Smith's Rest has around 1200 full-time residents and is a popular tourist location. On the weekends, families might drive up from the city to pan for gold just how they did in the 1860s. The town is rich with historical landmarks but the history hides a dark past centred around its church, Breakthrough.*

*Breakthrough, who recently came under media scrutiny for their staunch opposition to the gay marriage plebiscite and their controversial views on abortion, birth control and women's rights, has become better known in recent times for another scary trend: bullying and harassment of former members and those who 'enable' members to leave the church. It wasn't always like this in Smith's Rest.*

*Of those first settlers in the town, a few families remain. One is mine. I'm a descendent of an original family. Another is the Yule family, including Tim J. Yule, whose father founded the church in the sixties. Tim J. Yule now leads the church. Controversially, members must give up ten per cent of their income and over the years Breakthrough has accumulated significant stores of wealth. Yule personally owns dozens of properties in Smith's Rest, as well as in other parts of the state. Some of that money also goes toward employing members to conduct full-time surveillance on defectors.*

*What appears to be a quaint rural village from the outside is something else entirely just below the surface. Almost everyone in town is affiliated with Breakthrough. The church, which follows a fundamentalist reading of the Old Testament, hold beliefs that many would consider outdated. In my view, this church is incompatible with a modern Australia. Although they take their cues from the old book, they use very modern surveillance methods to pursue and harass those who defect, including me. After I left the church, I was pursued first by my family then by other church leaders. I landed in the city and soon realised that I was being followed, and my movements monitored. I discovered that friends I had made had been intimidated and questioned by members of the church. They contacted my colleagues, friends, partners.*

*And things didn't change for me at all until I contacted the police. According to the police their activity was legal, though only just, and didn't technically constitute harassment. The harassment slowed down – I guess the police warned them – but it didn't stop. I changed how I looked, I moved house, I deleted all of my social media accounts. Only now, years later, do I manage to live a normal life without the fear of being watched. I know they've done this with others who have left, as it is part of the church's ethos. They believe they're helping. They believe Satan has lured me and others away and so it's their duty to God to bring us back.*

*Religious groups are also not subject to the same tax laws as other organisations in this country. Given the predatory nature of Breakthrough, and the fact that members are manipulated into giving over ten per cent of their earnings, I'm still gobsmacked to hear that everything they do is legal. The church is Yule's personal bank, and he took from it to employ the people who made my life hell for years. I just hope someone with the power to change this, and crack down on rogue churches who operate more like cults, has the backbone to do something about it.*

Could this be what's happening? Could Samuel and Jessica have run away together to hide out? This explains so much about Jessica: why she doesn't have social media, why she is so private and barely touches alcohol – though she hasn't done anything major to change her appearance in the time I've known her. I send the article to Reid, and in a moment my phone pings again.

*I know. Lots of churches in the states operate in this way. Don't get me started on conversion therapy.*

Then a moment later, another message.

*I'm heading to Jessica's apartment now to investigate further.*

He mustn't confront her, he mustn't knock down her door to get to Samuel. This is where I need to step in.

I shoot a message back. *What's the address? I'll go myself.*

*Are you sure?*

I think about that article again. Jessica said she was still a believer, so what if she's taken him somewhere to be converted now that he's a father to her child? I can't wait to figure this out. I must act now.

*Yes. Please. I'll go right now.*

The moment the address appears on my phone, I'm out the door. I now know where she lives, and I have her phone number. Time to get to the bottom of this.

# TEN

SHE LIVES ON Collins Street, right in the heart of the business district. I stare at her phone number and draw all my nerves right into the centre of my chest, breathing deeply. I decide to dial the number.

As it rings, my trepidation grows. When I hear the click of the phone as she answers, it reaches fever pitch. Before I can say a word, she's already speaking.

'Leave us alone!' she screams down the line.

'Wait, Jessica, just—'

The line goes dead. I call back but she doesn't answer. I call Samuel's phone but it's turned off. I scan Reid's email again, my eyes settling on Jessica's address. It's not too far from here. It would probably take me an hour or so to walk there. I'm not sure what sort of reception I will get from her after the phone call, but I can't just sit around waiting to hear from Samuel. I *need* to know.

It's a warm day and by the time I arrive at her apartment building I can feel the moist heat of sweat between my shoulder blades and at the backs of my knees. I wait near the corner, not far from the entrance. After some time, someone leaves. I rush to the door, catching it before it closes. Her apartment is 609, which means it's likely a few stories up at least. I call for the lift but when it comes, I realise it won't take me up without a fob to scan. I just stand and wait, and soon enough, the elevator is called to the ninth floor. I get out as someone else gets in. I find the stairs and descend three flights, emerging onto level six. It's not hard to find, apartment 609. What will I say if he opens the door? How can I explain this? I just need to know that he is here. I raise my hand, steady my breath and knock. Nothing. A moment turns into a minute and still no-one comes to the door. I press my ear against it, listening. I can hear talking on the other side. Someone is in there. I knock again.

Then suddenly the door opens.

'Hello?' the girl says. It's not Jessica. A young Asian woman, with a phone pressed to her chest. She puts a mask on. I've interrupted her call.

'Sorry, I might have the wrong place. I'm looking for Jessica.'

'Why do you want Jessica?'

'You know her?'

A tiny vertical line appears right in the centre of her forehead. 'Sorry, who are you?'

I feel heat rushing to my cheeks. 'I'm just a . . . a friend. I was hoping to speak with her.'

'Right, well, she's not home.'

'You're her roommate?'

'Mmm-hmm.'

'Oh, of course. Do you know when she will be back?'

She just shrugs. 'She's always out for an hour or two in the middle of the day.'

'Same time every day?' I ask.

The crease on her forehead deepens. 'Look, I'm on the phone, and we're not supposed to have visitors in lockdown so . . .'

'One last thing, is Samuel here?'

Her face seems to relax, and I can see by the way her eyes shine that it's almost like she's holding back a smile. Then she shakes her head a little. 'No, Samuel is not here, actually.' I realise if there was a smile beneath that mask it was a sarcastic one. 'Why would Samuel be here?'

'I thought maybe he was staying here.'

'You're his mum.'

'I am,' I say.

She holds the phone in one hand and clamps her other hand on her hip, leaning against the door frame. 'Did he tell you he was staying here?'

I swallow. 'Um—'

'I've heard *all* about you. Your son is not here, he has no reason to be here, and I hope I never see him again.'

'Sorry?'

'Not after the way he's been treating her. I'm the one who has to comfort her when she's upset.' A pause now. 'I'm sorry but I'm still on the phone, your son is not here.'

'Um, sure. Okay, can I ask—'

The door closes.

I exhale. What did she mean? My son would never treat Jessica badly. He's upset her . . . how?

I can hear her murmuring into the phone on the other side of the door. I don't wait around. I walk all the way back to my apartment, reliving that conversation in my head and hoping I'm not fined by the police for being out for more than an hour. I get to the door of my apartment building, unlock it and slip inside. But right as the door is closing, I hear a voice. I push the door shut behind me and turn to see her through the glass, standing there. The woman with the black hair and the black mask – but now I see blue eyes. She raises her hand. She's speaking but with the mask and the closed door I can't hear her words.

I just stare at her, my heart pounding. Then she reaches up and lowers her mask. I see a face I recognise. Different hair but the same peach-coloured lips and electric blue eyes. It's her. Jessica.

We're not allowed to let people inside; that's the easiest way to get a fine. If one of my neighbours saw and called the tip line, I'd be in trouble. But I can't think about that now.

I open the door, look out past her.

'Come on,' I say. 'Quick.'

She looks around her, her eyes wide.

Then she strides forward, slips past me into the building and rushes up the steps to the door of our apartment. She's definitely not pregnant, and based on the look of her, she hasn't had a baby anytime recently either.

# ELEVEN

IF I'D KNOWN I'd be having a visitor, I would have tidied up a little. There are wine bottles seemingly on every surface, and the ashtray is overflowing. Moo has that lorikeet in her mouth again, barely recognisable now, with stuffing coming out and one eye missing. Dishes fill the sink as if the drain has been projectile-vomiting pots, plates and pans. My clothes are on the couch and the TV is still running the midday infomercials. Isn't this always the way? We don't see ourselves and how we are until we look through someone else's eyes.

'Sorry about the mess,' I say, because I need to fill the silence. I shift my clothes from the couch. Jessica has her mask back on.

'Don't worry about that,' I say, taking my own mask off.

She lets her mask hang from one ear. She's cut and dyed her beautiful blonde hair. I think about the article again. She's disguising herself. There's no baby but there's something else. And whatever it is somehow seems much, much worse.

'Take a seat.'

'Thanks for letting me in,' she says. Her voice is meek and a little sad.

'I was scared. I didn't realise you had dyed your hair. You give a bit of a Morticia Addams vibe.'

'Who?'

'The Addams Family?' Blank stare. 'Never mind. You're probably too young.' I go to the kettle, put it on the burner. 'Tea?'

'Yes, please,' she says. 'I dyed it a few weeks ago, and my flatmate cut it for me.'

'It suits you,' I lie. It makes her look like a goth. But I suspect she didn't dye it for how it looks.

'Thanks,' she says, staring down at her hands.

'So,' I say, setting her teacup on the coffee table and sitting across from her on one of the dining chairs. 'This is obviously about Samuel.'

'I'm sorry to just turn up,' she says. 'I've been trying to bump into you outside at that park for days. Samuel always said you went for your walks at lunchtime and I thought sooner or later I would catch you . . . or even maybe him.'

*Or him?* So she thinks he is here with me. 'You almost did,' I say. 'Sorry, I didn't know it was you. I ran away.'

'So he's not here?'

'No,' I say. 'I thought he was with you. That's what he told me.'

Jessica looks troubled. 'He told me he was staying here. He said he can't risk a fine so we can't see each other.'

I try to remember his words: did he say he was staying *with* her or *at* her home? If it was the latter, he might have meant her family home, but I can't remember. I think of Bluerazoo11 again, the taxidermy. It's creepy. I rise and go to Moo, who drops the lorikeet. I take it and put it straight in the bin, feeling her eyes on me.

'Sorry,' I say, going back to the living room. 'That thing was gross. So did he say anything else?'

She looks like she is going to be sick. 'No, he's only sent me the one message.' She clears her throat. 'Megan, my housemate, sent me a text message too. She said you went to my apartment.'

'I was desperate.'

'No, it's fine. I wish that we'd been in touch earlier.'

'I called you.'

She looks up now. 'That was you?'

'Yes. It was. You hung up on me.'

'I thought you were someone else.'

'Who? You sounded quite upset.'

Her gaze shifts to the window. 'Oh, um—'

'Your family?'

Now her eyes shift back to me, widening with fear. 'He told you?'

'No,' I say. My mind is whirring, Samuel must know something, a secret she wanted to keep from me. 'No, I guessed. It's a long story. Tell me what's happened.'

'I've decided to distance myself from my family—'

'*Distance* yourself?'

'Well,' she says, pausing to draw a breath. Her eyes fall on her hands resting in her lap. 'They're very religious and I'm not. Not anymore. They've been calling me day and night for the past couple of months. Members of the church have come to try to take me home, they've followed me. The lockdowns have been good in a way to stop them. Dad even came down to Melbourne himself and wanted me to move home for a "spiritual realignment". He said it was a mistake letting me go to such a corrupt institution as a university. He told me I had been brainwashed against him.'

'Did they speak with Samuel?'

Her look tells me all I need to know.

'Right,' I say. 'Why didn't he tell me?'

'I made him promise not to tell anyone. I just didn't want people to know about my family and all the religious stuff.'

'So your family, the church, is harassing you. That's why you're off social media? That's why you dyed your hair?'

It's all making sense now.

'I know what you're thinking. They're not dangerous or anything, it was just easier this way. I thought it would help to stop them. They're not bad people, they just believe something different to everyone else and it's from a place of love.'

She sounds just like every other young woman defending her abusers after she has been manipulated, gaslit. She still loves her family, that much is clear. Even if she no longer believes what they do. I see a single tear spill from her eye and have the urge to hug her, but I need more answers.

'Now that they can't come down, they just harass you from afar?'

'The members call from different numbers and every time I answer they try to talk me into coming back. I just hang up most of the time. I need to change my number, but if I do then Samuel won't know how to contact me.'

'How long has it been going for?'

She bites her lips for a moment before speaking. 'I think they realised something was off when they found out I had a boyfriend. Then they saw a video on Sam's vlog of him talking about his atheism. That's when it all started and they wanted me to come home.'

'And how did they know you were with Samuel in the first place?'

She shrugs. 'I was always careful because I knew how my dad would react to me dating a . . . heathen.'

I think about her fake smiles in Samuel's photos. She was worried, even back then, about someone posting them online. Now I do move closer and reach out to give her a hug. She bristles at first, before letting me hold her. Her body shudders.

'Shh,' I say. 'It's okay.'

'I just want him back,' she says. 'I want this to be over.'

I rub her back for a moment before speaking again.

'Jessica, I need you to answer one question for me. Do you think . . . is it possible that Samuel is with someone from your family or the church? For any reason?'

She gently pushes me away. 'No,' she says. 'The church wouldn't interfere in that way. He wouldn't go with them either.'

*But what if they took him?* I think. 'I read an article online from someone who escaped the church. It sounded scary. It sounded like they went to extreme lengths. If there's any chance they're involved in this . . . I mean, could they have coerced him? Or lured him?'

'No,' she says. 'I can call my father. I don't want to, but I can.'

I know I'm putting her in an awkward position.

'Do you think your father blames Samuel for your change of heart?'

'Maybe. I mean, he probably does. I know they contacted him.'

I don't say what I'm thinking. That this might be enough to have set her father off. Maybe he wants to convert Samuel, thinking it would bring her back to them.

She speaks again. 'They don't kidnap people.'

But does she really know that? Does she understand how dangerous and fanatical people on the fringes can become?

'Okay,' I say. 'I was certain that . . .' I shrug, suddenly embarrassed by the idea. 'I thought maybe you . . .' I don't say *were pregnant.* I change tack. 'Your roommate said you've been upset. Did he do something?'

'I haven't heard from him, that's why I came here. He won't answer my calls, he won't message me back, and I just feel so let down. He was different the past couple of weeks. And since the lockdown, he's sent only one or two messages . . . We normally speak and message all day, every day.'

That sick empty feeling intensifies. He hasn't been with her. He's been lying to me. But why?

'If it makes you feel better, I haven't heard from him much either,' I say.

'I think there's someone else. I've had this sick feeling for weeks that he was seeing another girl.'

'What do you mean?'

'He's been messaging someone else and he would go out and see them, then when I asked him who he'd been with he would just say he'd been out with his dad. Stuff like that. But I knew he wasn't close with his dad.'

I want to tell her that Samuel doesn't lie, but I'm beginning to realise that maybe I don't know Samuel as well as I thought. He's been keeping a secret from both of us.

'Was he talking to someone else online?'

'I think so. I don't know who it was. I didn't find out. He was using an anonymous messaging service. It could have been anyone.'

'And he was meeting this person? You're sure?'

'I'm not one hundred per cent sure. It's just that he would disappear for a couple of hours, then come back to my apartment.'

'Well, thanks for telling me. When I hear from him, I'll make sure he calls you, okay? He's not normally like this.'

'Maybe he is with Marko?' she asks.

'Marko says he isn't,' I say. And why wouldn't Samuel just tell me that? And why would Marko lie about it?

'Anyway, I have this,' she says, opening her bag. 'I didn't see anything on there, and I know he wasn't communicating with his friend on email, but I can leave it with you. You might see something I missed.' She pulls out his laptop and places it on the coffee table. 'He left it at mine.'

He hasn't got his laptop. He must be using someone else's.

'Thank you,' I say. 'I'm sure it will be a big help. Oh, and one last thing. Do you know anyone who does taxidermy?'

'Taxidermy?' she says, her eyes rising to the ceiling. 'No. No-one springs to mind.'

•

After Jessica has gone, I message Reid to let him know that Samuel is not with her. Then I phone Marko, but he doesn't answer so I message him instead.

*Is he with you, Marko? Jessica said he was heading to see you that day. I need to know. This better not be some game you're playing.*

But why would Samuel be in on it? Why would he lie to me? I hear the ringtone of a video call coming from my bedroom and I go to it like a shot. It's him. Samuel. I answer, wait for the screen to load, the connection to establish. Then I see him staring out at me. The first thing I notice is his head. His hair . . . it's gone. I blink hard at the screen as if it's a filter, or something on the lens of his camera is obscuring his beautiful hair. But I can see his bluish scalp, no hair at all. He's shaved it off. For the first time since he was a newborn, I can really see the shape of his skull and a sickly dread pours over me: Bluerazoo11, the photo of the hair in the dirt, the animals. It's him. That's who has my son. My heart is pounding in my chest. It's the same person who liked all my images. They wanted me to see their profile.

'Mum,' he says, his voice not quite as buoyant as usual. 'Hi.'

'What's going on, Samuel? Where's your hair?' I try to keep my tone even.

'Oh, this,' he says, running his hand over it. The sound is a rasp. 'Yeah, freshening up for summer. I've never shaved my head and thought what better time than lockdown since I'm not going to see anyone for a little while anyway. What do you think?'

'It looks good,' I tell him. It looks awful, like a prisoner, but I don't share my honest opinion.

'Um, so, anyway, I just spoke with Dad.'

'Oh,' I say. 'How is he?'

'Well, I think you would know, Ma,' he says. 'You've been in contact with him a lot lately, he said.'

'Yeah,' I say, my eyes sliding away from the screen for a second. 'I've been a bit worried.' What else is there to say? The tension is a dam, on the brink of bursting.

'He said you thought I had disappeared, or something had happened to me. Is that true?'

'I was worried at first, yes, of course I was. You know that.'

'But he said you still think I'm in trouble?'

'You've not helped to allay my fears, Samuel. Every time I talk to you, there's something else. And do you know anything about some Bluerazoo11?'

His eyes go wide at this, but after a moment he shakes his head. 'Ah, no. That doesn't ring a bell.' There's another long pause here, I think the camera must be frozen, then he speaks again. 'Look I'm sorry for being hopeless with my phone and not telling you I was with Jessica, but you can see I'm fine now, right? You can see nothing has happened to me.'

I just shrug.

'Please stop worrying, Ma.'

I eye him, study the dark bags beneath his eyes. That scalp scraped clean of hair. What would he say if I told him Jessica was here, in this apartment just a short time ago? 'Are you really fine, Samuel?'

He still has this habit from when he was just a boy, lodging his tongue in his cheek and frowning when he is thinking. He does it now, his eyes aimed at something beside the screen. Then he looks back at me. 'I am fine, Mum. Perfectly safe and happy. Please stop scaring Dad.'

'I know you're not with Jessica, Samuel. You never lie.'

He rubs at his eye for a moment. Lets his breath out. It doesn't look like he's slept all week. 'Mum, why don't you believe me?'

'Jessica was here, Samuel. She just left—' I stop speaking because on the screen now I see his finger come to his lips, his eyes filling with fear.

He leans a little closer, lowers his voice. 'I'm somewhere else.'

'Where?' I say. A sound behind him. The shriek of metal sliding open. Then a flash of action. The door slams. He swivels in his seat toward a man striding across the room with a balaclava over his head.

'Samuel?' I say, my voice urgent and breathy with fear. 'Samuel!'

But he's looking back at the man. The man wears a singlet, and I see lean stringy arms, with a faded tattoo of a lorikeet on his tanned forearm.

'What—'

But the man is past him now, near the computer. Before anyone can get another word out, the internet cuts. The screen freezes. My heart slams.

'Samuel?' I ask the blank screen. Then something pops up.

*How would you rate the quality of this call?*

'Shit!' I say. 'Shit, shit, shit.'

*Would you like to save the recording?*

Yes, of course I would. But mainly I want to speak to my son. I want to call back first. He's in trouble. Who was that? Who was with him?

I try to call him again but it doesn't ring. My heart is racing.

'Come on, Samuel, what happened? Where are you?' I say out loud to myself. *Who was that man? What is he doing with my son?* I'm already reaching for my phone and dialling triple zero, but I pause with my finger over the call button. That tattoo . . . I've seen it somewhere before, *but where?* In a newspaper article?

No, I think, no, it can't be. It was a tattoo of the same bird, the rainbow lorikeet. The one Moo destroyed.

I watch the recording back. Pausing when the man enters the room. His posture suggests anger. I'm shaking with fear for my son. He looks at Samuel like he might murder him. Then past him, his eyes rest on me, on the screen, for just a split second before he rushes forward. I imagine he's gone to where the internet is plugged in. He snatched it out of the wall to end the call. Going back and watching it once more, with a growing clot of dread in my chest, I realise the man entered right as Samuel told me he wasn't at Jessica's apartment. Just as he was about to tell me where he is. Samuel lowers his voice and shifts his eyes to the side. Then the door flies open. It's as if this man was listening on the other side, waiting for Samuel to say something.

I send the recording to Reid, then watch it again and again, like a horror film, and the anxiety grows each time. I was waiting for him to tell me the truth about what's going on. I was so close. My eyes fix on that tattoo.

My email pings.

*Just saw the recording. Call me when you can.*

*Reid.*

I call him immediately.

'What should I do? Phone the police?'

'You should call them, report him missing and think about sending in the recordings. This is serious. You need the police right now.'

'Could you find out who the man is?' I ask. But I think I already know. I'm sure it's him.

'I'm stumped, it doesn't look like Jessica's father. Do you have any ideas?'

'No,' I lie. 'No, I don't know.' But while I speak, I pull up images from the news articles from all those years ago. I search for his face, but there's nothing. Just a brief description of what happened. No pictures, so I can't see any tattoos, but I'm sure I've seen it before. I try Facebook now, but again I can't see the tattoo.

'Just call the police and tell them everything you know,' Reid says.

I'm not going to do that.

'I just want to be a good mother,' I say. 'I just want to protect him. Now someone has him. Do you think they're hurting him?'

'My default setting is to assume the worst and hope for the best.'

'And how can we figure out where he is exactly? I'll go there myself.'

'There aren't really any clues on the video footage, so short of tracking his phone there's little I can do. You wouldn't happen to have his log-in information for Apple? Or he's not sharing his location with you?' He makes a sound somewhere between a laugh and a sigh.

'I wish,' I say. 'No, I don't have access to his account and he doesn't have his location shared with me but I do have his laptop from Jessica now, so I will let you know what I find.'

'Go phone the cops. Check out the laptop. I'll do what I can at my end and let's talk again soon.'

The moment the call ends, I realise that I haven't mentioned the Instagram page to Reid. I check it now. Bluerazoo11. Another post is up. He has zero followers so I'm probably the only one who is seeing this. A video. I feel cold and exposed. The video is of me, sitting out on the balcony with a cigarette between my fingers, drinking wine. He must have recorded me from across the road in the park. I don't know when it was recorded, it could have been a while ago or it could have been yesterday. I don't know which is worse, if it was days or weeks or months. But it doesn't matter in the end, the point is he's clearly given this a lot of thought. Another post comes up, this time it's of Marko dragging his bins out to the roadside. He's in a white shirt and brown slacks. Both have the same caption. I rush to the bathroom, lean over and heave. Throwing up for the second time in days. I think about the caption.

*I know what you did. Now it's time to pay.*

# TWELVE

I STRAIGHTEN, HOLD my stomach. He's taunting me. I lean under the faucet, suck up a mouthful of water. I go out to the balcony, look over the park. I don't see anyone watching me but I feel exposed. This is some cruel game, and now that I think I know who it is, we can't involve the police. I open Samuel's laptop. The battery is flat but I soon find the charger in his room. It boots up and I find his email logged in. I scroll through the messages. It's almost entirely stuff about university coursework. One message screams: *See your matches!* It looks like it's from a dating site and it was sent just five or six weeks ago. *But he was with Jessica then.* Maybe that's it. Maybe that's how this man lured Samuel away. He might have started a relationship with him online, catfishing him with photos of a beautiful woman. I let my imagination go, but I know it's unrealistic. Samuel was too honest for that. He wouldn't cheat on Jessica.

I call Marko.

'What do you know, Marko?' I ask as soon as he answers.

'What?'

'About Samuel. Did you know he was with that man?'

'No,' he says. 'What are you saying?'

'I'm saying Samuel told Jessica he was going to see you, and he also told me that. Then he disappears.'

'Wait – what man?'

'I spoke with Samuel, and there was a man in a balaclava who came into the room. He had a tattoo of a lorikeet on his forearm. It was faded but I could see it clearly.'

A long pause. 'What does that mean?'

'I've seen it somewhere before. It might be *him*. I think it is him. I remember seeing it on his arm, it's faded now but it's the same. And this Instagram account started following me. Bluerazoo11. Check it out. There's a video of us. He knows where we live, who we are.'

A few moments pass. I imagine his face changing, from a little annoyed to disgusted and finally afraid.

'If this is your idea of a joke, Lou—'

'Of course it's not a joke. Someone has him. I'm telling you.'

'How would he be able to figure out who we are when the police couldn't even do it?'

'I don't know. Maybe Samuel figured it out? All I know is he's in trouble. *We're* in trouble.'

'I had a note in the mail a couple of days ago. *Who took Samuel?*' he says. 'I should have told you but I was convinced it was from you.'

'What?' I say, trying to keep the anger out of my voice. 'Why didn't you tell me? How could you keep that from me?'

'Because you were acting unhinged, Lou. You sounded desperate enough to do that, to send me the note to try make me believe something was wrong.'

'Maybe . . . maybe we should call the police, maybe we could go down to the station. They might understand. You can break curfew to report a serious crime—'

'No fucking way, Lou. No. Out of the question, don't even suggest it.'

'Well, we can't do this alone. We need to find him. We need to!' It's getting dark outside.

A long pause. 'I've got a mate, Nolan, who I play golf with. He's a copper. He won't ask questions.'

'How well do you know him?'

'He's one of my best mates, we play most weekends. Or we did when we weren't locked down. He's got me out of a spot of hot water before with speeding fines. Look, I'll just speak to him. I'll be careful. But we can't tell any other cops anything.'

'And he won't go digging into the past? It's historical, but it's still a serious crime.'

'Just let me handle it, alright.' He's losing his cool. 'If it is him, Lou, we're in deep trouble either way.'

'Okay,' I say. 'Okay, just, please, I'm serious Marko. I just want Samuel home . . . he must be so scared.'

'Don't do anything until you hear from me, okay?' he says.

Then he's gone.

# THIRTEEN

THERE'S NO POINT trying to sleep when I'm this wired, so I just sit there dizzy with fatigue, waiting for something to happen. Then, all at once after a few hours, I drop off like a zapped fly.

It seems only a few minutes have passed when a ringtone obliterates the silence. I jerk suddenly, violently awake but am still disoriented by echoes of the dream world overlaying the dark room around me. I'd dreamt Samuel had decided to move out, and that he hated Marko and me. He wouldn't listen to reason, he just kept screaming in my face. There is only one light source in the room and it's my phone, still ringing. I reach for it and see his name: *Samuel*. Just like that night I had the two missed calls. Only now, I'm awake for it and I'm flooded with relief. It's in my blood like a drug, like that hit of nicotine when I drag on the first cigarette of the day.

'Samuel,' I whisper into the handset. 'Are you okay?'

'Mum,' he says. The line's bad and his voice is low and urgent. 'I don't have long.'

'What's going on, Samuel? I'm so scared for you. I'm losing my mind here.'

'I know, I know. I'm sorry,' he says, his voice a rushed hiss. 'I shouldn't have come. I never should have come here. I'm so scared.'

'Where are you?'

I hear him swallow. There are no discernible sounds in the background. 'I don't know, Mum. He drove, I got in the car and I wish I hadn't.' I can tell he's crying now and I just want to hold him.

'Oh, Samuel, how did you meet this person?'

'It's a long story . . . I did—'

He drops out again. 'Samuel, I can't hear you.'

'—there was going to be a curfew. Then I thought I couldn't get back—show them my licence and they would see. Worst case scenario, I get a fine. But then—'

'Samuel, you are cutting out?'

'I'm sorry, Mum. I messed up and now I'm stuck. He won't let me leave.' His voice gets smaller; it sounds so quiet, so brittle that it could break at any moment. 'I snuck into his room for my phone.'

'Where are you? I'll come get you.'

'I don't—the exact address—somewhere on Laird Station Road.'

'*Laird Station Road?* That's not in the city.'

'Why did I get in the car?' he says, crying again now.

'Do you have a number for the house?'

'No—near the end—property.'

'Who is it? Who is he?'

'He said you and Dad—'

I hear something down the line again. A crack. Like a gunshot. I freeze, concentrating on the sound.

'Son?' I say. 'Samuel, are you there?'

'I'm here. I jus—He told me he's—'

'What was that sound?'

'I don't know, I don't know.'

'You sound scared, Samuel.'

'I need to get back inside—before he—tomorrow.'

'What would he do if he found you?'

'—a gun. I'm scared—'

Rage swells up inside me.

'He has a gun? Samuel—'

The line goes dead.

I can't describe the feeling inside. It's everything at once, the prickle of terror, that horror and fear for my son. It's after 2 am and my body trembles with fatigue but I can't sleep. I won't sleep.

Back during those night shifts at the airport, standing in my cushioned black shoes with the endless lines of tourists, caffeine got me through the night. But now it's not caffeine in my blood keeping me alert. It's unspent raw adrenaline and all of the new information from the past few days running through my mind.

What was the street name? *Laird Station Road.* Nothing comes up when I search it. It's wrong, or I misheard.

There's a sound in the room, a heaving breath. It's coming from me, deep inside. I feel sick and dizzy. I close my eyes and try to relax but anxious tension is filling my limbs. My head is swimming. Despite my initial instincts to involve the police, I know it's too risky for Marko and me. If the person behind this is who I think it is, the man from all those years ago, then it's best we keep the police out of it. He must know that too.

I have two text messages from Reid, but before I can open them I hear a buzzing and my entire body goes tense, my heart slamming harder still inside my chest. It's the intercom – someone is downstairs at the door and the sound tears through the silence of the apartment. I feel the itch of fear hot on my skin. We are in curfew; no-one should be out. So who is it? Who is ringing my buzzer at this time of the morning, risking fine and arrest? Could it be him, Bluerazoo11? The cops are monitoring the roads, which makes me wonder how they got here.

It rings again. I go to the intercom and on the screen I see someone out on the street. It's not the police, it's someone else breaking curfew. He stands just at the edge of the camera's view. My hand trembles as I reach and press the answer button.

'Hello?' I say, the nerves rattling my voice. 'Hello?'

No answer. He's standing far back in the darkness with a mask on. Can he hear me?

'What do you want?' I say.

He doesn't answer. He raises his arm, and curls his hand toward him, calling me down. Gesturing for me to come closer.

Air is trapped in my throat. On the intercom screen, he's still standing there. I'm reminded of that awful horror film Samuel made me watch. It gave me nightmares for weeks. The girl who climbs out of the TV with dark hair hanging over her face. I feel a chill rushing over me again, just thinking about it. And now, here is this man, face half-covered in a mask and a pale hand calling me to him. In the darkness, the screen is black and white but when he steps closer the security light comes on. Squinting, I realise it's Marko.

My breath is still rushed and heavy. I know what I've got to do. I go down the stairs slowly. He won't be able to get past the locked front door, so I can just approach and see what it is he wants. Why didn't he call? *I'm safe,* I tell myself, then I whisper it: 'I'm safe.' So why is my heart thudding so hard? I get down the steps and start toward the door but as I get close, I see he's not there anymore. I have that odd sensation that I'm being watched, that he's here somewhere in the foyer. I quickly glance around. No sign of him. Then I see, just tucked in away from the light, the shape of my ex-husband. He's probably paranoid about being seen and reported for being out in curfew.

A chill runs over my skin. I breathe as deeply as I can and reach for the door, opening it just an inch before calling to him.

'Marko, what is it?'

'I came as quickly as I could,' he says, stepping forward now into the light.

'Why? What happened?'

'He sent me this.' He holds out his phone and I see a blue dot on a map. The nearest road is Geary Station Road. Not Laird, but close. 'That's where he is.'

'I spoke to him, Marko. He's in trouble. The man has a gun.'

His face goes pale and wind tears along the street.

'He could have gone to the police. If he knows what we did to him, he could report it, but he didn't. He's choosing to do this to us.' Blood is pumping in my ears. He's right. 'We could just . . . Look, he's baiting us.'

'What are you saying? That we leave Samuel with him? That we cut and run? He's our son, Marko. He's *ours*.'

He can't meet my eyes. 'And did you see his latest post?'

'Which one?'

He shows me on his phone. It's a picture of a man with a hood over his head. *Samuel*, I think. It's him. Pointed at his face is the barrel of a rifle and the caption reads, *Come get him, bring $50,000 cash, no police.* I feel like I might throw up.

I look up into Marko's eyes and see something I've not seen in almost two decades. I see he is afraid.

'I have half the money,' he says. 'I had a few thousand in the safe at home. So I went to three different ATMs but it's the best I can do, and I had to call the bank to increase my withdrawal limit.'

'We have to go to the police, Marko. I don't care anymore. He's in danger.' We have to do it for Samuel. We have to give ourselves up.

'No,' he says. 'We will both go to jail, Lou. You know it as well as I do. He won't hurt him. This is about us, not Samuel.' He clears his throat. 'He won't hurt the boy.'

His logic doesn't work and we both know it, but I want to believe he's right.

'So what do we do?'

'There's a location on the post.'

He shows me. It's out in the country somewhere. 'It's an hour and a half's drive.' It's not Smith's Rest. This has nothing to do with Jessica or her father. We know exactly what this is about and who is involved. And it's clear what we must do. I think about Reid, his directive to call the police, his messages. He might have figured out where Samuel is too but we are in this alone.

'We do it together,' he says. 'We finish this thing once and for all.'

'What if he's told other people?'

'Well, we can't control that but it looks like he's just as keen to keep the cops out of this as us.'

'So,' I say, 'my car or yours?'

He thinks about this for a moment. I've still got the car we had from when we broke up. A Mitsubishi Pajero with 300,000 clicks on the clock. We had put his car in storage. Soon after Samuel arrived, we got the Pajero and wrecked my old blue Toyota. 'If we get stopped, it will be a disaster. We'd be sent home or arrested. Neither option works.'

'Well, we have to take that risk.'

'I think we can mitigate the risk, though. My mate, the cop, he said they're spread pretty thin. They're not monitoring all roads.'

'Right.'

'I think we should take two cars. I'll take the eastern freeway then cut along High Street through Thomastown on the way out. You take the Westgate Bridge then avoid arterial roads until you're out past Melton. If one of us gets caught, the other can go ahead, and if we both make it out of the city then we can meet up closer to the place.'

It's a good plan, and it makes sense, but if Marko is stopped I don't think I'll be able to go it alone.

'Okay,' I say. 'I suppose that's the best way to approach it.'

'Here,' he says, handing me an envelope. 'It's half the money, a quarter of what he asked for, but that way you'll have *something* if I get stopped.'

They know where I live. They have my son. If I go to the police, we will both go to prison. Everyone will know what happened and Samuel will still be gone. I feel sick as I go back upstairs and get my keys and a jumper before heading to my car. I unlock it and climb inside. Marko has already set out, racing off into the night because he has the longer route ahead. We'll talk through a plan on our phones as we drive.

Before I depart, I delete Reid's text messages without reading them, and then block his number. Then I listen to the recording of Samuel's call again. I focus, squeezing my eyes and every sinew in my body to hear his final words as the line dropped out. The reception must be bad in that part of the country. Worst of all, Samuel knows what happened. He knows the truth.

# PART TWO

PART TWO

# FOURTEEN

'WHAT IF THERE'S more than one of them?' I say into the speaker phone as Marko answers the phone.

'More than one?'

'Just because it seems like Samuel is with a man, it doesn't mean the man is alone.'

'It doesn't really change anything,' Marko says. 'He knows we're coming. If it's him or twenty others, it doesn't matter. Samuel is there, he wants us to come, and he wants the money. We need to end this.'

'How could we be so stupid? This was always going to happen. We rode our luck all this time. We got complacent.'

'It's not the time to apportion blame,' he says with a hint of annoyance. 'We have a deal.'

'You drove the car,' I say. 'You drove us home. You could have stopped.'

'I know I did. I know. I've regretted it every day since. But *you* didn't give me much choice.'

I exhale. He's right. But I don't say this. Another thought occurs to me. 'What if we can't stop it from coming out? Maybe there's a way you can still live your life.'

I want Marko to know that my life, my responsibilities, aren't the same as his. Maybe if it all goes pear-shaped, I could take the fall alone. I need to be there for Samuel, but if push comes to shove, if both of us are facing going down, then maybe it could be just me.

'What are you saying?' he asks. 'We were both there. I drove the car, right? I took us home. We've both lied and covered it up all this time.'

'Well, we'll just have to cut this guy a deal. Hopefully the money is enough. Maybe I'll leave it locked in the boot until we have Samuel.'

'Let's meet at the top of the road before we go in, okay?'

'Sure,' I say. The wet road hums beneath the tyres.

'I'll see you there. Top of the road.'

I hang up the phone and dig my fingertips into the hard leather of the steering wheel.

# SAMUEL

FOUR NIGHTS. THAT'S how long he's kept me here. Four nights since he lured me away from the city and trapped me in this old farmhouse that creaks in the wind. With all these cats skulking about. I'm watched over by a man who drinks twice as much as Mum and has become increasingly controlling. He smokes pot and says, 'I hope you don't mind. It's the only thing that helps me sleep.' And when he'd fallen asleep and I'd fetched my phone, he found me with it, grabbed it back then crushed it with an axe. He said I should be grateful; he said it's *them* who took *everything* from him, and then he drilled a padlock onto the door of the shed and locked me away. I should have just run away, that was my chance to escape, but now it's gone.

'I'll put them in prison, then you'll have nothing. Do you not understand what they did?' he asked. 'Do you understand how easy it would be for me to completely ruin their life? Her and that prick don't deserve to walk the face of the planet after what they did. They ruined my life; it's only fair I ruin theirs. You're mine now, you need to understand that.'

It's not about me, I realised. It's about revenge.

It's very late or very early. I haven't slept, I've just been lying here, still and terrified, knowing at any moment he could come in here. I've been thinking about how I could run away. The road is not so far, but then what? It's so quiet out here and how would I get out of this shed anyway? During the day, I hear one or maybe two cars in the distance, but I couldn't get away without him noticing. Even when he's in the shower, it's so quick, and the first thing he does when he gets out is check on me.

I know he's telling me the truth about what happened, which makes Mum and Dad liars. It makes them bad, bad people. She always told me to tell the truth. She told me it's impossible to live a happy life with a dark secret. But I didn't realise that all this time she's been speaking from experience.

# FIFTEEN

IT'S HARD NOT to speed, knowing Samuel is in trouble, knowing every passing second could bring him more pain and fear and suffering. Would he really hurt him? It's only us he wants.

The map tells me it will take an hour more to get there. Then we'll demand that he hands Samuel over in exchange for the money and that will be it. It's not $50,000 but it's a lot and what could he expect with such short notice? If that's all it takes to end this, then it'll be worth every penny.

The road stretches out in front of me. The wine from earlier is mostly out of my system now and the adrenaline of the sudden decision is starting to wear off. I must stay the course, though. I can't turn back and there's no room for indecision. I'll go there and I'll get him out, one way or another. The time flies by and soon the maps are directing me down a long country road. It occurs to me that Marko's motivation is probably different to mine. He's coming to make sure he doesn't go to prison. It's a callous thought, but I know it's true. He cares more about himself than Samuel.

Before long I'm pulling over near an old rust-chewed sign that says *Geary Station Road*.

Marko was right. My phone has no signal and there's nothing but the darkness to calm my nerves. I find a radio station playing easy listening through the graveyard shift. No ads or radio hosts, just gentle music. And it seems to work in distracting me a little.

I don't know how this will go down. But I would do anything for Samuel. That's something this man probably doesn't understand; he probably doesn't realise how strong our connection is.

Soon headlights turn onto the road, pulling in behind me. Now my heart slams so hard it almost makes me feel weak.

It's Marko, coming closer. I drop the window.

'Here,' he says, holding out an envelope thick with what I assume is the cash. The other $12,500.

'Put it under your seat. He'll assume it's in my car. Leave it here and we can drive up together. When we see Samuel is safe, after we make sure he isn't going to tell anyone what happened, we can let him know where the cash is.'

'What if he wants all of the money before releasing him?'

Marko thinks for a second. 'I guess I will offer to transfer the rest.'

'Are you sure he just wants cash?'

'Well, what else? Samuel? Us? I think he knows the situation he's in. We've both broken the law now. And besides, we would have heard from him or the police if it was anything else.'

I swallow and nod. 'Do you think he told Samuel?'

'That doesn't really matter now. We can talk to him about it after.'

I feel sick just imagining what Samuel will say. I block it out; that's a problem to fix later.

In Marko's car, I try to steady my breathing.

'I've turned on location services. If anything happens to me, the police will be able to map my phone here. This man must know he can't hurt us.'

'I'm not so sure. He seems unhinged.'

'Well, I have a back-up plan,' he says.

'A back-up plan?'

He sighs. 'Only if things don't go how we planned.'

Marko drives with his headlights off all the way along the road, slow and cautious, leaning forward to peer through the darkness. There are almost no houses on the road and after a few bends and a descent over the hill I see the number 170. This is the place.

'Here,' I say.

'You sure?'

'It says 170.'

He turns in slowly, the wheels are achingly loud, crunching on the gravel.

The house ahead is dark, as we roll slowly along the driveway, the dust whispering against the tyres.

'I guess I'll just park beside the house.'

'Not too close,' I say.

He stops a few car lengths from the front of the farm shack. My heart is pounding against my sternum.

'Alright,' he says. 'We'll tell him we have the money, but we won't give it to him until we get an agreement that this is the end of it.'

'Yeah,' I say, my trembling breath giving the word vibrato. 'You do the talking.'

'Let's go.'

We open our doors slowly. We step outside. Suddenly there's an explosion. I drop to the dirt, cover my head and scream.

'Took your time, didn't youse,' a man says. I look at the house, the dark of the doorway. He's standing there, shotgun in hand. 'Where's the money?'

My pulse is racing, and my limbs feel like jelly. I look up and see the barrel of a shotgun pointed at my head. I let out another scream, but I know no-one is coming to help us. All the properties are too far away. He knows this too, that's why he feels he can just blast his shotgun into the sky.

'We've got it,' Marko says, breathlessly. 'Just put the gun down.'

'Stand up and give it to me.'

Marko, I realise now, is crouched down on the other side of the car.

'I'm not going to do anything until you put the gun down.'

I hear his boots, then glance in his direction as he walks down the steps toward the car. 'Is that so?' he says. Then he laughs and points the gun at my ex-husband. 'I think you're going to do exactly what I say.'

Marko stands now, puts his hands up. He turns his head as if bracing for a blow. 'Okay. We've got it, but we can't give it to you until we come to an agreement.'

'An agreement?'

'This is the end of it. He's grown up now. We're sorry, okay. It was a mistake, but you have to understand we were desperate. You can't keep just keep Samuel, he's eighteen.'

He laughs. 'Samuel? Is that what you call him. Go on,' the man says, waving the gun toward the house. 'Inside, both of you. You're not going anywhere until I have that money, my compensation. And the boy is staying here with me.'

BEFORE

# SIXTEEN

THERE WAS NOTHING an ambulance or a doctor could do. I knew that the very moment I found him, and the last thing I wanted was for them to take him away. When Marko got home, he sprinted to the bedroom.

'How far off is the ambulance?'

I shook my head. 'I didn't call.'

'Shit, Lou!' Then he was off back out to the kitchen. I got to him as he was dialling, reaching out and pulling the cable from the phone base attached to the wall.

'What are you doing?' he said, his eyes wide with panic, fury, grief.

'He's dead, Marko. Anyone can see that. He's dead and he's not coming back.'

His eyes narrowed. 'I'm calling an ambulance!'

'Just let me have some time with him. They can't save him now. It's over.' Another wave of grief hit me and I collapsed there on the floor. Marko came down with me, holding me. We'd saved so much, and spent it all doing IVF over and over. Our lives had been on hold for years and by that stage I'd stopped counting the miscarriages. I'd almost given up hope when the last round of IVF worked and made it past that twelve-week scan we so dreaded. We'd both cried. I'd never seen Marko with tears in his eyes until that moment, and then that evening in the birthing suite. We had a son; he had come very early, but he was alive, a mewling pink infant, and he was perfect.

Then, just a few weeks later, in his cot in our room, I found him. For the first time, he'd slept through the night. I was so fatigued, so mentally drained, that I managed to sleep through too. Except I discovered he hadn't been sleeping. Marko left that morning for his early start; he'd snuck out quietly not to wake him, or me. When I found him face down in his crib, he was so cold, so blue around the lips, with a tiny crust of vomit on the cot sheet. I just stood holding him to me, howling. I called Marko, he raced home.

I wanted to die. I'd never felt that before. I would have hurled myself from the roof of a building. I thought about the painkillers in the cupboard; I could chew them all up. I wanted to give up on this cruel world and go with him. I was completely drained of every feeling but a chest-crushing grief. I wanted all the drugs and alcohol I could get, to go out with a bang. I wanted it to all end in a black hole of anaesthesia.

Hysterical, I talked Marko into keeping him at home; we didn't want them to take him away to bury him just yet. I knew rationally that it was unhealthy, that he was going to begin to decompose. Having him there would stop being a comfort and would eventually become a horror. But deep inside I knew I wasn't ready – that if they took him away and embalmed him, if the police asked all their questions about the death, I wouldn't survive because then it would be real. Our baby would be dead forever. It's illegal to take more than twenty-four hours to report a death but I didn't care. I just wanted him close; I wanted to keep him.

That year had been so hard. There was the night Marko had hit the cyclist. He was tense all day, certain he was going to be arrested at any moment. Then finally we had the good news that the pregnancy had taken, but while I swelled up, Marko's paranoia heightened. He installed security cameras. He had cash in a bag and was ready to flee. He thought the man in the hospital might die. We only had my little blue Toyota because his car was locked away in storage. We took it out of the city, down the peninsula to a beach near where I grew up. We'd decided on that third day we would report the death and have a proper funeral to bury him. I knew I wasn't ready to say goodbye, but Marko was going to hold me, he was going to help me get through it. I thought about that statistic, everyone knows it, the one about marriages after the loss of a child. They almost never last. I knew my grief was bigger than our love and the cracks were already showing. He didn't want Samuel's tiny body in the house anymore; he thought we needed to start to do the formal stuff, the funeral and burial. He thought we should get out of the house, and that's how we ended up at the beach. It's not rational, but that's what grief does.

We watched the monstrous surf down below from the car park on top of the cliff. It was salt in the wound when I saw that woman holding her newborn. I saw the life we could have had. But their towels were surrounded by empty beer cans and I recognised her, even from that distance. *Cassie*. Last I heard she had been kicked out of her parents' home for stealing things to sell to her dealer. We had done swimming together at high school, although she was the year below me. She was an addict yet there she was with a little baby. I remembered a night at the Espy in St Kilda when she'd looked after me, the night the creep had groped me. I remembered crying and feeling her arm around me. But she was a different girl back then.

On the beach, she laid the baby down in that basket and the envy bubbled over. I thought I would go at that moment and throw myself in the sea. I would end it. I couldn't stop watching them. Then she got up, crossed the sand to the water and dove in.

It seemed to me so selfish, so strange, that a mother could not be with her baby all of the time. She was thin, too thin to be a new mum and the baby was tiny. Cassie was flighty, troubled at school. In with the wrong crowd and, despite the fact she was clever, you could always tell she was going down the wrong path. I'd heard the rumours and seen the track marks. She'd tried to cover them up with a tattoo. A rainbow lorikeet on her forearm.

She was with some guy who was a little older and was also into drugs. She'd been on the periphery of the party scene, into ecstasy, speed, then eventually heroin. She had become addicted. Now she was being reckless.

The only moments I had ever been away from my baby was when we put him down for his naps. I'd *never* do something so irresponsible, and yet I was the one with the dead baby. Anyone with half a brain could see the risks: the surf was too big to swim, but worse still was the rip and she was walking straight into it. Without lifeguards on the beach, it seemed obvious what was going to happen. When Cassie started to drift out further, I saw the man get up.

'She's in trouble,' Marko said, leaning forward over the steering wheel.

I thought he might try to be the hero, run down to the water to save her.

'He's going out too,' Marko said. I saw the father making a decision and I felt so much anger, so much pain. He looked around, his eyes searching the beach, then up toward us. No-one could help him. He took the surfboard and ran toward the sea. He was choosing his wife over his baby. Yes, she'd been swept out; yes, she was struggling, but how could they be so irresponsible? They didn't deserve that precious, helpless thing.

'What about the child?' I said, turning to Marko. I could see dark rings under his eyes, the way his mouth hung slightly open. Mourning our baby had taken it out of him too.

'What child?' Marko responded, his eyes fixed on the rescue. I realised all eyes were on her. Of the few people on the beach, not one of them was looking at anything other than Cassie, struggling against the surf, and her boyfriend rushing into the rip.

It was a heady cocktail of anger and jealousy, spiked with the sleepless rage and injustice of our own situation. I was driven by these things, but it was something else too. Love. The promise of a life where I am a mother, where my son, Samuel, didn't die. I would be the best mum a boy could have. It was a delusion, but I could see our life coming back. The life we always wanted. It was someone else's turn to go through the pain. I *deserved* it more than her. The decision made itself. I knew I didn't have much time. I opened the door.

'Lou,' Marko said. 'You can't help.'

'I know her,' I said. 'She was an addict.'

I ran down the path to the beach. I got all the way to their things, then I picked up the baby, a boy, just like we'd had. He was sleeping, so peaceful and still. Older than Samuel but not by much. I held him for a moment. I thought I would just cuddle him, see how I felt. I thought that would be enough. Maybe I would scold the parents for leaving their baby behind, maybe I would talk to Cassie and somehow she would let me take him. No. It wasn't going to work that way. I realised these two were no more deserving than me and Marko. In that fugue state, I made a decision. If it was a little girl I'd found down there, what would I have done? I often wonder about it. It would have muddied the waters a little.

The decision would have been much more complex. Calmly I started back over the sand. I carried the baby all the way to the car, opened the door then got in.

'What the hell are you doing, Lou?'

'Go,' I said. 'Start the car.'

'No, I'm not going anywhere.'

'You don't want to go to jail.'

'That's why I'm not starting the car.'

'Unit 432, 174 Station Street, Pakenham.'

'What is that?'

'That's the address of the storage facility your car is in.'

'What are you saying?'

The baby began to wake, crying and reaching out. I opened my top and it easily found my breast. I was surprised to feel the tug of his mouth as it closed over my nipple. *It's meant to be,* I thought. Like Cinderella's shoe.

Down below I could see Cassie almost at the shore on the surfboard and the man, with those strong shoulders, was battling through the surf on his way back in.

'I'm saying it's not fair what happened to us. This is a way out. We have a baby, Marko. And if you don't start that car I will tell the police exactly where they can find the vehicle that was involved in that hit and run, and they'll know that you were drunk.' I steadied my breathing. 'These people will never know what happened to their son; that's a blessing. On the other hand, our son will always be dead. This is a way to have *something* after everything we've been through. They can have another baby; *we* can't.'

I saw his Adam's apple bob up and down. 'This is serious, Lou. Someone might have seen us. You can't just snatch a kid off a beach.'

'No,' I said. 'We just got here. No-one has seen us. We haven't left the car. No-one will remember. We drive straight back, we make a plan. We'll be home before night.'

I looked down. I could see the woman by the basket. Her hands on her head, she looked up toward the car.

Marko shook his head, biting his bottom lip. 'It's not right.'

'Start the car!'

Marko exhaled. He reached forward and turned the key.

'We have a secret. That's it. We will forget and live with this.' My heart was pounding as he turned that little blue Toyota around. 'It's fate, Marko. No-one has really met Samuel, and babies change so much. No-one will know.'

'I won't be able to live with this,' he said. 'This is something else entirely, Lou.'

We got back to the house. Marko made a tiny coffin out of balsa wood. Together we placed Samuel inside, weeping as our new baby clung to my chest, his chubby arms capped with fists, and blinking those perfect little eyes. Then Marko dug a hole in the backyard.

'It's deep enough,' I said.

But he kept going, each blow angrier than the last.

'You'll hit a water main,' I warned, holding the new Samuel against my chest. 'Then what? How would we explain this hole?'

But he didn't stop. Not until his entire six-foot frame could fit inside.

I wept. He was stoic. We said a few words. We gave the new baby Samuel's name. I watched the news of the daylight kidnapping. There were theories about an animal taking it, echoes of the dingo story. There were theories that Cassie's family might have been involved. I kept checking throughout the day and all of the night, searching for any hint of anything out there that could link us to the case. I watched the police giving statements. Marko couldn't stomach it, but I made myself sit through the desperate pleas from Cassie. It broke my heart, but it reminded me of the sacrifice, of what I was prepared to endure, to be a mother for my baby. I knew he would have a better, happier and safer life with us. As the story died down, as the vigils ended, we continued.

We went about our life. For a few months we missed our appointments with the maternal child health nurse, always coming up with excuses and ringing in his measurements and weight. We didn't get his vaccines until he was almost two, just in case someone noticed something off or recognised him, but the more we took him out and realised no-one looked twice, the more I began to feel the coils of tension inside relax. By then, he looked so different to the images circulating that no-one ever thought the normal well-adjusted couple in the nice neighbourhood could have taken the baby from the beach.

Then Marko left.

It wasn't so bad. It had been coming for a long time. And I knew we were both bound to Samuel. I knew he wouldn't abandon him, he wouldn't let him have a bad life; he owed it to Samuel to be a good father. But his heart wasn't in it in the way a father's heart should be. It wasn't like with his new kids and his new wife and her functional womb. It was obligatory; for eighteen years, he paid child support for a mistake he'd made.

I raised Samuel better than those two ever could have. I never let him out of my sight and while I was teaching him baby sign language, then later getting him into advanced mathematics classes after school, and driving him to piano lessons, his *real* parents were using again. While I was raising a morally sound, smart and honest boy, their lives were spiralling back to how they used to be. Wasn't it better for everyone this way? Especially Samuel? He was much more clever, much better-looking and kinder than Marko and I ever were. He has had an amazing life.

Some time ago, I stopped following what Cassie was up to. Samuel was born before social media really took over our attention, it was just something you checked from time to time like opening your letterbox.

Then I heard about the overdose. That's when I started to drink more. That's when the guilt started to get the better of me.

Now I see that the perfect crime doesn't exist. You can never dig a hole deep enough to bury the past entirely.

# SAMUEL

IT STARTED THROUGH the app. Heredity – one of those services where you send in your DNA and they send back your ethnic make-up and promise to unlock the family histories hidden in your genetic code. A lecturer at university suggested if we were interested in doing it, then it's a fun and easy way to learn about real-life applications of genetics. There was one thing the app did that I didn't expect: it shows you all the matches from your DNA. Those in the system who are related to you, and how they are related. When I set up the profile, I clicked the box that says *Allow matches to contact you*. I thought, *What's the worst that could happen?*

I discovered my ethnic make-up, and it was surprising. My dad claimed to have strong Polish ancestry and my mother always joked that her grandparents were more British than Earl Grey tea. But what I found was no Polish ancestry at all. Just sundry British and European countries highlighted on the tiny map of the world. I thought, *Well, Dad is in for a rude shock when I tell him about this*, but then I got an email.

*Would you like to see your new matches?*

It was odd, but it was odder still when I clicked to see who they were, and it came up with two names I'd never heard of before. But their location checked out: *Victoria, Australia.* Odder still, under *How you are related*, I saw *Mother 99.9%* and *Father 99.9%.* My first instinct was that Mum and Dad had done the test under fake names. You never know, this data could end up in anyone's hands, so maybe it was a privacy concern. I kicked myself for not using a fake name too. But soon a message had come through and my world tipped on its axis.

*I've been looking for you for eighteen years.*

I froze. Can you imagine living your entire life believing you are one person, then discovering that it's all been a lie? I didn't believe it, not at first. I thought there must have been a mistake. But when he told me about the beach kidnapping, and then when I read about it in old articles online, I knew he was telling the truth. The story checked out and DNA doesn't lie, even if everyone in my life did. I was angry and confused, but I still loved my parents, or had strong feelings of loyalty to them, especially to my mum – or Lou, I guess I should call her now. I know what she has sacrificed for me. They gave me a good life, even though they were separated. And she loves me more than anything in the world.

But. I continued the conversation with this man online, and started to find I couldn't look at Mum in the same way. At times, my anger threatened to overwhelm me. I thought of all the birthdays and Christmases she'd made special; I remembered the fact she'd picked up extra shifts at the airport to help put me through private school. She cooked and cleaned and did everything for me. But did that undo the fact she took me from another family? Did that exonerate her of kidnapping? It occurred to me that maybe it was someone else who took me. Maybe they got me through some illegal adoption service. I wanted so badly to believe Lou was incapable of taking someone else's baby. Marko, maybe, but not Lou. So I asked her if they would have adopted. I pressed her on it but she never confessed to anything; she didn't show any hint that I was anything other than her biological son.

My real dad and I have spoken a lot over the last few weeks. I learnt the full story of his life and I learnt what happened to my mother. He said he was always so proud that she chose him. She could have had anyone with her looks and her big brains. But she was sick. She was hooked on drugs.

They stayed together for about four years after I went missing. They always hoped I would return somehow, but the relationship was broken, and they started to have fights; sometimes the fight would end in a stalemate where they separated for weeks and he would have to collect her from some rundown house in Richmond, with bowls of used needles on the kitchen bench and bare mattresses on the floor. He'd drag her away, kicking and screaming. He didn't sugar-coat it. My mother was an addict. He'd been one too, he admitted. He told me they both did horrible things to feed their addictions.

At one point, when they were both managing to keep clean, they'd heard the story of a woman in the States finding her father online via a DNA service called Heredity. This was fourteen years ago, when the service was still quite new. So they submitted their DNA to Heredity and all other similar online services. My birth father said that his father had paid for it all. He was working at a car wash but he was also breaking into cars in nice suburbs at night. They never expected the websites to work but it felt like their only shot as the police seemed to have given up on finding their son. After nothing happened, he told me that my mother finally gave up too, and he knew what was coming. It felt inevitable. The stability that came when I was born was violently torn away when I was kidnapped, and she never got it back. She went through highs and lows; her parents put her into rehab and she came out the other side balanced again, but it didn't last. My birth mother accidentally overdosed thirteen years ago, that was the official cause of death, but my birth father told me he knew it was a suicide. She'd planned it out. She couldn't go on.

Before she died, they'd been to see a police task force that deals with child exploitation material. They were made to flick through a book of screenshots of kids' faces from child pornography, but I was just a baby when they last saw me. Sometimes they thought they recognised me, but they couldn't be sure, and that just made it worse. He said it was the most excruciating experience of his life because he knew that when most children are taken, they are hurt and exploited in this way. Then every time a child victim turned up, every time there was a breaking news story, whenever the police contacted him, they had a spark of hope that would instantly be extinguished when they realised it wasn't me.

He said my birth mum took her life in the car park overlooking the beach where I was kidnapped. By that stage, they had been broken up for months. He got the phone call from his mother-in-law, my birth grandmother. The needle was still in my birth mum's arm.

When he asked me to meet in person, it was like it was a final step for him to see that I was real. He told me that he just wanted to see me and to talk.

'You're an adult now. There's no reason for me to be in your life, but I feel like I'm owed this by the universe. I want to see you with my own eyes. Now that Cass is dead and so much time has passed.'

I didn't think twice. I was nervous, of course, but it almost sounded like he forgave my parents.

'You're not going to call the police, have Lou and Marko arrested?'

'No, Samuel. Why would I? For all I know, she adopted you. Maybe she paid someone for a baby? And if she goes to prison, where will you live? From your stories, she seems like a good lady.'

He wasn't what I was expecting. He seemed much older than Marko, taller but stooped in a way that made me think gravity was riding him more than everyone else. His skin was sun-damaged, and he wore a leather jacket like a bikie but there was no patch on the back.

He sat down across from me.

'I can't believe it,' he said. 'Can I give ye a hug?'

I nodded. Seeing the joy in his eyes, I thought I might cry myself. I stood and he came around the table. He held me for so long I thought other people at the cafe must be watching. I could smell cheap men's spray and shampoo. He had impossibly white straight teeth which I realised were too perfect to be real.

Then he sat down again and smiled, all teary eyes. 'You're a good-looking bastard,' he said. 'That's from her.'

That was how it started. He was so curious about my life, also about Lou. He wanted to know everything about her and Marko. He told me about his hobbies. He was a hunter; he lived off the land on his dusty farm in the country. He told me about his taxidermy, bringing little critters back to life as he called it. It was a way to distract his mind. He gave me a lorikeet just like his tattoo; it was impressive, so lifelike, and it stood up on its own.

Then I met him again the day the lockdown happened. I hadn't heard the news and when he offered to show me his farm and see some old photos of my birth mother, how could I say no? I didn't have the full story of who took me from that beach, and I didn't have the courage just yet to confront Lou. I wasn't sure if I ever would.

I climbed into his old Ford that droned like an aeroplane and we listened to the Rolling Stones and he told me about his childhood and his life up until that day on the beach. We passed through the small town of Clunes, with wide streets and colonial-style shopfronts. It had a good feel to it, like somewhere I could visit again and again. When we got to the farm, I noted the road name, but soon forgot it. Then we got to the house. I didn't check my phone at all for missed calls or messages; I didn't care if Lou and Marko were worried. I didn't even care about Jessica in that moment. I just wanted to keep going through all his old photos and his memories. He was unlocking a part of my history I didn't even realise had been hidden from me. It was like discovering a secret cave under the house you'd lived in all your life, a place of magic and wonder.

Then quite abruptly he said, 'You can sleep here tonight if you want. Do you ever stay at your girlfriend's? Your folks would think you're there with her, right?'

I felt sick. I didn't want to let him down, but the city was a two-hour drive away and it was already dark.

'I think I need to get back,' I said.

'Well, it might be tricky, actually. I just saw the news and there's a curfew. We won't get you back in time.'

I laughed and then I saw a cloud cross his face. I stopped laughing.

'I think you should stay the night, see if you like it. I've got clothes, a new toothbrush, everything.'

He tossed a bag toward me and when I looked inside, I saw a few t-shirts and shorts, all still with their tags on. 'My computer,'

I said, my voice slow and stomach queasy, realising he'd planned this enough to buy me clothes. 'I need it for my coursework.'

'I got one you can use,' he said. 'It's a bit old but it does the trick. I have the internet hooked up and all.'

He'd charged my phone but when I reached for it, I found I had no reception. I still didn't want to say no; I didn't want to let him down. After all, he was my birth father, and he clearly wanted to know everything about me.

'You can call your mum,' he said. 'Just tell her you're at a friend's house, or say you're with your girlfriend. She doesn't need to know, especially, you know, if she really was the one who kidnapped you.'

That first night, I didn't call her. He said out in the paddock sometimes you could get enough coverage to get a phone call through. He didn't have a landline and would need to find the cable for the computer. He said he would do that in the morning but for now he just wanted to have a drink with me. I felt guilty as we drained cans of beer out on his porch; he'd crush each one in his fist and toss them toward the door when he finished. We looked out at the country, the night sky and the symphony of rural sounds. Mosquitos feasted on me, but after a few beers I stopped noticing them.

I knew I couldn't leave. I felt trapped, and thinking about Mum at home worrying made me sick. I told myself one night away wouldn't hurt though. I'd get back to her tomorrow and explain. She would think I was with Jessica anyway.

I could barely keep up with him drinking beers, but soon enough we were both drunk and he kept talking and I kept listening, the guilt slowly easing as the night went on and the stars came out.

He told me he and my real mother loved the beach, but when I was taken, they had to move, and he can't be anywhere near the sea anymore because it makes him so angry, he gets a headache. After a couple of days when he barely let me out of his sight, I began to realise he wasn't going to let me leave. Then he told me what he was planning to do. He said he's seen the big house Marko lived in, that he knew he'd be good for a bit of money. And after he got the money, he was going to put a bullet in both of their heads. Then he was going to drive us away, deep into the country, to start again. He told me I would learn to love him, after we got to know each other. I told him we could just run away; he didn't need to kill them.

'They gotta pay,' he said. 'They're gonna pay and there's not a damn thing you can do about it. So you might as well accept it. They're not really your family. They ruined my life, Cassie's life and they ruined yours. Made you soft but we will toughen you up.'

NOW

# SEVENTEEN

'YOU KNOW,' HE says. 'There are parts of this country where you can disappear. You can get a new name, rent a little shack out in the middle of nowhere and be someone else. That's what I'm going to do when we're done here.'

He hasn't bound us, or even threatened us, he's just made us sit across from him at the round table, with the gun about half a foot from his right hand. *Could I leap across the table for the gun?*

We're in some kind of shack, all wood with naked bulbs and an old TV in the corner. But hadn't Samuel been kept somewhere with bricks behind him? Maybe it was another building on the property.

'Please,' I say. 'Please let us—'

'I don't want to gag you, but I will,' he says, his voice firm. 'I'd seen you in old photos, I know you were friends. But then everyone seemed to go their own way. Addiction is a disease, and when Cass got sick, you all disappeared. So just imagine my surprise when your son told me your name, the same Lou who had been at school with Cass. That's when I knew it was deliberate, it was planned.'

He exhales, then stands and goes to the fridge, taking the gun. He pulls out a can of beer and wedges the gun under his arm, freeing his hand to open it. He sits again, taking a mouthful. 'You know she was clean for her pregnancy; well, from when she found out she was pregnant anyway. And she was doing well after that. She didn't even want to drink or anything because she loved him so much, I couldn't believe it. I kicked the stuff too. It was easier for me, but then I never got as deep in the hole as her. I found her in that dark place and the baby – Chase he was called – well, Chase pulled her out.'

He slams his fist down on the table and his nostrils flare. 'She needed something to take her mind off the fact her baby had been taken. She needed a hit, and I let her have one. You never *became* his mother when you took him away. You just killed his real mother. You understand that? How can you live with yourselves?'

I didn't know. It was so easy to imagine that she was still using, that Samuel's life would be horrible with this woman. It was so easy to pretend I had saved him.

'I'm sorry,' I say. Then I begin to cry. 'I'm really sorry, okay, but this isn't going to bring her back. Nothing will bring her back. This is just creating more suffering. Where is he? Where is Samuel?'

'CHASE!' he roars. 'His goddamn name is Chase and if you say Samuel one more time I'm going to spray your brains all over that wall.'

'I'm sorry,' I say again, my voice cracking under the pressure of my terror. 'I'm sorry. Chase.'

'Say it again.'

'Chase.'

'Now you,' he says to Marko.

'Chase,' he says. 'Chase. That's his name.'

'That's right. Now where's the money? You better—'

'Look,' Marko says, interrupting. 'It's not exactly what you think.'

'How did I know you were going to say that? I just knew. Where's the money, Marko? Show me the money.'

'Where is he? Where is Chase?' I say.

'He's not leaving. And neither are you.' He takes the gun and points it at Marko's head, so close it's almost touching.

Marko's breath grows loud and hoarse.

'Don't kill us. Please. Look, I don't mind, you keep him here, but before I give you the money, I need to know this is the end of it.'

'Of what?'

'The secret. The fact she took him from the beach.'

'She?'

'Yeah, she,' he says. 'I just want to give you the money and go back to my family and you can keep the boy.'

*She took him.* Is he blaming me alone? Before the moment of confusion passes, before I can speak, the man cuts in.

'You think you can just leave, after what you did? You think I'm just going to sit here and thank you for fifty grand after you ruined my life? An eye for an eye, Marko. So here's how it's going to go. I'm going to shoot you and when she sees what this here gun can do to a human head, she's going to take me to where the money is.'

Marko's eyes shift to me then back to the man. 'Okay, listen. The money is in her car, it's under the driver's seat. But you don't need to kill us, not *both* of us.'

*Both of us.* It takes a few seconds for the words to sink in.

The man smiles. 'Both,' he says, savouring it. 'What are you saying, Marko?'

'I didn't take him. I had nothing to do with it.'

'You expect me to believe that?'

'She was grieving after we lost our baby; we went through hell. Then she just turned up at home with another baby. I didn't ask questions; she told me it was just some dodgy adoption service. I didn't realise it was your baby until months later when I saw a news story and by that stage I was implicated.'

'Is this true?' he says to me.

But Marko answers first. 'She'll lie. But it's the honest truth. I told her to come forward but she kept threatening me, saying she would tell the police *I* took the baby.'

*He's lying through his teeth.* This is what he does. He's an excellent salesman and he's using his skill set now to try save himself. I did force his hand, but it's because he hit that cyclist. And he was there that day. I didn't just turn up.

'I don't care about the boy, I didn't even want to come here,' he says.

The man turns to me, steps back and swings the shot gun in my direction.

'No,' I say.

'You stole him, and blackmailed your husband?'

'It's not true. He's making it up. It didn't happen that way.' I eye Marko. 'Lying isn't going to save us!'

'Outside,' he says. 'Both of you.'

'She did it, she'll lie to get out of anything, she will throw anyone under the bus. She probably followed you to the beach; it might have been planned. I don't know. She knew Cassie, like you said.'

The man narrows his eyes.

'So you did plan it?' I can see a vein in his throat. I study his eyes, searching for tells like I used to at the airport. I thought he might have been on something, but now I'm beginning to think he's just buzzing on adrenaline and anger. It's a potent concoction, and I sense that anything can happen. So why is he talking to me? Why isn't he doing something? What if he's waiting for someone else?

'No,' I say.

'Well, who is going to get it first? It's you or him and right now I believe him. You knew her.'

I step back, raising my hands. 'No,' I say again. But the shotgun comes up, pointed right at my chest.

Marko does nothing to help. He just stands there. 'It was her, I had nothing to do with it.'

'She just turned up with the baby?' the man says.

'That's right. I didn't know he'd been kidnapped.'

The man smiles now. The muscle in his left forearm bulges as he grips the gun tighter. I close my eyes and tense everything. This is it. Tears squeeze out. I brace for what I know is coming.

# EIGHTEEN

'WAIT,' I SAY, desperation distorting my voice. I make a decision.
I can't die like this. I think about Samuel. I need to survive this
for him, to save him. 'Wait, I can prove he's lying. Let me show
you. It's on my phone.'

I open my eyes a little, see the gun staring back at me.

'Prove it?' he says. 'How?'

'It's on my phone.' I open my eyes fully now, but still my entire
body is tense.

'Where is it?'

'In my pocket.'

'Put it on the table.'

I move slowly, while he keeps the gun trained on me. I place it
on the table and step back again. Finally the shotgun comes down,
but he still holds it in one hand.

He reaches out. 'Passcode?'

'0909.'

He unlocks it. 'There's an app that records my calls. It's called VidSafe, or something like that. Listen to the most recent one. It's with Marko.'

Marko's face changes, his eyes go to the door. He pulls his hands out of the pockets of his hoody.

The man holds the phone to his ear, his eyes on me first, then slowly they slide across the room to Marko, his expression changing.

I hear a fragment of our conversation.

*You drove the car. You didn't need to, but you drove us home. You could have stopped.*

*I know I did. I know. I've regretted it every day since. But you didn't give me much choice.*

I watch the man's face slowly morphing from confusion to white rage. 'You lying bastard,' he says. 'I hate when people lie.' His cheeks go a shade past red, almost purple.

'Please, I have a family. She has nothing!' Marko pleads.

'You *have* a family? I *had* a family!' he roars. He lifts the gun.

Marko flies at the man. He throws a looping punch and it connects. He tries to pull the gun away but the man takes one hand off and lands a sickening uppercut that rocks Marko's head back, sending him stumbling back in a daze.

Marko rushes at the man again, unsteady now, and this time when he lashes out he misses. The butt of the shotgun catches him and he's sent sprawling. Marko rolls, then looks up at the gun pointed at his head.

He raises his hands. I slip behind the man, he glances back, and in that moment Marko is back up on his feet and out the front door.

'Shit,' the man says, going after him. There are sounds of a tussle, punches landing. Then I hear a voice.

'No!' It's Marko. 'Please,' he begs.

That's when I hear an explosion that shatters the quiet of the night. I don't have much time. There's another shot, equally loud. *Marko.* I can't just leave him. This feeling surprises me a little. He is such a selfish bastard. But I know I have to help. He's in trouble. The footsteps are coming back toward the house. I rush out the backdoor right as the man comes in.

'Don't run,' he calls out. 'It'll just make it worse. I want the money, then you can go. That's all I want. Just the fifty grand.'

I don't speak. I can't.

'Give me your keys, then you can go. I know it was him now.'

He's lying. I run around the outside of the house. I could run into the paddocks and try to hide but the urge to get to Marko is too strong. He might have gotten away but maybe he's hurt.

When I get round to the front of the house, I see light coming through the open front door. He's close behind me and I can't stop. Then I see him. Marko's on the ground making a gurgling sound. I can't look but I can't look away either. The shotgun blast looks like a shark bite, tearing most of his shoulder away and the left half of his jaw. I let a sob out. His eyes are just slits and there's blood, so much blood.

'Marko,' I say. 'Please don't die, please.' But I know already he won't survive. Footsteps are coming round the side of the house.

'Where are ya?' he says. 'Come on, stop playing games. I need those keys. Then you can take the boy home and move on. Nothing to be done for ya lying ex, though.'

*Nothing to be done.* This man is a psychopath. He shot Marko. He's killed him. I breathe in hard, stiffening my resolve. *You're surviving this, Lou. You're going to save Samuel and escape.*

I go back into the kitchen silently as he hunts for me outside; I open drawers, searching. I find a knife; it's a large knife and it's my only chance. I find a plate and hurl it across the room so it smashes through the window on the far side.

'You bitch, what are you doing?'

Boots running up the steps. He's coming. I've got to be ready. I brace myself, draw a breath and pull my arm back, tucked in behind the door.

The gun barrel enters first. Then he steps inside. I swing the knife as hard as I can, stabbing at his chest. The knife hits something, and it seems to bend against my palm. I stab again. It's wet and warm, the blood rushing over my hand. The barrel swings. Another explosion, right beside my ear.

His fist snatches my shirt front, and we fall down with my ears screaming from the blast, and my body electric. The gun clatters to the ground and the knife slips out of my hand. His blood flows onto me.

'You . . . ruined . . . my . . . life.' He squeezes the words out one at a time through gritted teeth.

He pins me down, then reaches for the knife.

'Samuel!' I scream.

'His name is Chase!'

'Samuel! Help me!'

He draws his arm back. It feels like a punch, right in the side. Then an explosion of pain radiates from my ribs.

'He's not coming to save you,' he says, close to my ear. 'He's my boy now.'

He's right. I'm going to die, I realise. This is how it ends. I'm surprised how much it hurts, the knife inside of me. I can barely breathe as he draws his hand back again, the point aimed at my throat. I lift my forearm and the blade hits, steel lancing through skin and flesh, slamming into my bone. More blood, but it's mostly his. He draws the blade back once more. I reach out in desperation and press my fingers into the gash in his chest. His face contorts. I dig them in deeper. I raise my knee hard into his groin and his grip on my other arm loosens. I twist my body. He falls against the table, clutching my wrist to pull my fingers away from the wound. The blood is pulsing out. I stand, step back. He tries to stand but loses his feet and falls on the table.

I take the knife and stab out again, this time below the ribs, hitting something softer. He falls back, holding the handle of the knife, his face a rictus of pain and shock. I step away slowly, keeping my eyes fixed on him until my spine hits a wall. I rush outside. He said Samuel was locked in the shed. I scream out into the night, clutching one hand to my side. I hear Samuel's voice come back from somewhere. There, ahead of me, is the shape of a small building. I run, tripping once in the dust. At the shed, I find the door is locked. Samuel is hammering away from the inside.

'It's me,' I say. 'It's Mum, I'm here.'

'Mum,' he says. The word is a balm. I feel it soothing me from within. I'm still his mum. I can hear the tears in his voice. 'He has a key. I can't get out.'

The key. I can't go back in there; I can't face him. I think of Marko again. He's dead and I'm dying. I need to get to a hospital.

'I'll come back,' I say. 'I'll save you, Samuel. I won't be long.' My voice is breathless and desperate. I go slowly, almost silently toward the house. Every step is torture, but I need to get the key and the blood is still flowing. How long can I go before I pass out? How much blood can a person lose?

With my hand pressed hard to the wound in my side, I trudge forward. Slowly I step through the door. Inside I find a pool of blood right where I left him. But he's not there. My heart leaps.

Then I turn and see him, the gun in one hand, heaving with each breath. He goes to raise the shotgun but can barely get it up to his shoulder. He falls back against the kitchen bench. He's sliding down with the gun still in his hand. It's my chance. I snatch at the knife, pulling it out of his chest.

My side screams with pain. I reach for the wound and press a hand to it once more, feeling the blood still flowing. The knife aches in my fist. I rush toward him. The gun comes up and he aims it right at my chest. I pause, gasp. I raise a hand as if it might stop what's coming.

He squeezes the trigger. There's no blast. The gun simply issues an impotent click. There are no shots left. He's coughing now, blood bubbling from his lips. I crawl to him as he tries to reload the gun, gripping the barrel and aiming it away. Then the knife goes in all the way to the handle, right in his stomach. He opens his mouth, his breaths short and sharp. I pull the gun and it comes loose from his grip. I toss it across the room. I push my hands into his pockets, feeling around until I find a set of keys. Bloody and battered, I take the keys back to the shed. My body is weak, and I feel dizzy. *Just open the door*, I tell myself. Then it will all be okay. I fumble with the padlock, get the key in and turn. The padlock comes free. The door opens and he's there. Just as I collapse.

# SAMUEL

I COULDN'T GO in the helicopter with her, but the police arrived soon after it took off. I saw the blood but I didn't go any closer. I just walked toward the driveway and sat down on the grass, waiting.

Since then, Mum has been in hospital for three nights, and not even I can visit her given the lockdown restrictions. I have called her every day though, and we had flowers delivered. Jessica has been staying at the apartment and together we watched the story on the news, the helicopter footage of the house I was in, the shed where he had kept me. It's all anyone is talking about on the morning shows and the evening news. My phone has been blowing up; mostly my friends calling, but sometimes journalists. I tell them the same things, reliving my time at the house, but I can't quite capture it in words. How surreal it all was. On the one hand, I wanted to get to know this man, he was my birth father.

But on the other, he locked me up, and manipulated me. It felt like so much longer than just four days, and the time before it happened feels like another life entirely. Everything changed and my world shifted when I discovered my parents are not who they said they were. *I* am not who they said I was. They stole me away but I can't ignore the fact that my birth parents might not have been able to give me the same level of care and opportunity I received. I would be a completely different person had they raised me. Would my birth mother have relapsed? Would they have stayed together? When children are kidnapped, they *never* end up in a good, loving home like I did.

Dad – Marko – was the hero who turned up and tried to save me, but that man killed him in cold blood. It's still painful, how much I miss him. He wasn't always there for me, but you grow up with a man you believe is your father, you learn from him and model your own masculinity on him. You learn about the world through him, then suddenly and cruelly in an instant he's gone.

There's just a few more weeks of lockdown then we will be free, and it couldn't be better timing. As the police piece things together, I hear the word *random* used more and more to describe my kidnapping. I know what will happen to Lou if the police get the full picture. Maybe it will come out. They will surely soon realise that the man who locked me in that shed lost his son to kidnappers almost twenty years ago. The police may even ascribe his criminal actions to the breakdown of his family, the years of drug use and alcoholism. But will they really make the connection to me? I doubt it. So unless he shared the secret with someone else, then I guess it won't come out. I've been thinking about it all. I can't stop thinking about it. It was so difficult, so uncomfortable, for Lou to live with the secret that I was kidnapped as a baby. She was speaking from experience all those times when she said I should never keep big, dark secrets because they rot you from the inside.

Maybe that's why she drinks so much. Either way, she was right. I know in my heart that only the truth can set you free.

When they interviewed me, I told the police just what I needed to: that I met him at a cafe, that he came and sat next to me. I said that he threatened me and made me go with him out into the country. I deleted my profile on Heredity and deleted the messages. I hoped they wouldn't be able to access his accounts, or our DNA records. I didn't tell them that we had met before that day in cafe. That we had been in contact for weeks. I thought I was doing the right thing by lying to protect Lou, but only now do I realise this makes me complicit. This is not how she raised me. The guilt will chew away at me and I will never reconnect with my grandparents or any of my real family, those who are left anyway. I will be just like her. I will inherit this secret and carry it around for the rest of my life. If I am a good person, if I am true to my upbringing, I know what I need to do.

Jessica is beside me on the couch.

'You don't have to do this,' she says.

'I do,' I say. 'I have to.'

The detective left a card after he interviewed me. Now I take it in my hand and punch the mobile number into my phone.

'Listen,' I say, when he answers. 'There's something else. Something I didn't mention.' Jessica squeezes my hand.

'What is it, Samuel?'

I hope Lou understands why I'm doing this. I'm sure Mum could say Marko instigated it or we could get her a good lawyer to negotiate her sentence. I just hope she understands this isn't a betrayal. She may not be proud of me when she finds out, but in the long run I'm sure she will come to see that this is how she raised me. To do what I know in my heart is the right thing. One day, she will be free again and she will be able to live unshackled by this awful thing she did in the past. Only then will she be truly free and maybe then she will come to see why I'm doing this.

'You still there?' the cop says.

'I'm here.'

'So what is it?'

'I need to tell you the truth. My name is Chase Adams and I was abducted when I was a newborn from Rye Back Beach eighteen years ago.'

# EPILOGUE

THERE WAS A gasp of time, a matter of days, when for the first time in nineteen years I was free. Unburdened from the lies, from the secrets I'd kept from Samuel, and still free in the world. But true freedom came when I accepted that Samuel knew. And the world *would* know. We hurt that cyclist; we took the baby on the beach. It was us. We ruined Cassie's life. Maybe we drove her back to using again, maybe she would still be alive today if not for us. Maybe Marko would still be alive if not for that day at the beach.

It's really not so bad inside the Dame, the correctional facility where I now live. What had terrified me most when I was charged was knowing I wouldn't be able to have a drink inside. But since then, something has changed. The hunger for a drink, to begin the slow anaesthetising march of booze, it was gone. The fog had cleared and despite being here in this prison, it felt like I had a second chance.

I was sentenced to five years but my lawyer says I'll be out in three if I keep my head down, express my remorse. People might think I'm angry with my son – I still see him as *my* son: I raised him, I gave him everything. But how can I be angry with him? In a way, he knew something I didn't – he knew I could only be truly free and happy if I faced up to what I did. And I know that the truth would have likely come out in the end anyway, with all the media and the police sniffing about. Someone would have made the connection. Before it came to that, Samuel did exactly what he was raised to do: he told the truth in spite of the consequences. How can I be anything other than proud of him?

When he first visited me in here, I could tell he was nervous. He couldn't look me in the eye at first.

'I'm so sorry I just—'

'You did *nothing* wrong, Samuel. No need to apologise,' I said, reaching out to touch his hands across the table.

'It's just I knew it was going to help you, I knew it was for the best—'

'You did what I should have done a long time ago. I should be thanking you.'

•

Sometimes at nights, when I'm lying on the hard mattress, listening to the disquiet of the cell block, I think about that day at the beach.

The way in an instant our lives can change. I try to imagine the younger me, how tough life was, how desperate I was to have a child. I read a lot in prison, and I've taken up playing chess with one of the other inmates, Margot. She's clever like my Samuel, she was a psychologist who snapped and did something quite horrible outside but I think she enjoys helping me, talking me through my issues. I have my chess, my friends inside, but I think more and more about that young Lou.

It's like I'm there, watching her in that car. I dream about it. The moment my life changed forever. We wanted so badly a normal family life. We wanted so badly to wind back the clock to before our baby had died to when our life was on track. I imagine the scene now: I'm there hovering in the back seat of the old blue Toyota. I lean forward and whisper into young Lou's ear. 'Don't think. Just do it.' I smile. 'It all works out in the end.'

# ACKNOWLEDGEMENTS

LIKE ALL THE other books I've written, I have a lot of people to thank for helping me write this one. In particular, thanks to Karen Yates, Bill Massey, Paige Pomare, Tania Mackenzie-Cooke, Mel Winder, Kate Stephenson, Jackie Tracy, Rebecca Saunders, Emily Lighezzolo, Emma Rafferty, Dan Lazaar, Pippa Masson, Gordon Wise, Jerry Kalajian, Lynn Yeowart, Tiffany Plummer, the Hachette Australia team and the Aotearoa Hachette team.

READ ON FOR AN EXCLUSIVE SNEAK PEEK
OF J.P. POMARE'S 2024 THRILLER,
*SEVENTEEN YEARS LATER*

# ONE

TK

HUMILIATION: THAT'S WHAT drove Bill Ruatara to stab each member of the Primrose family with his chef's knife. Or perhaps he did it because Simon Primrose withheld his final paycheque. Others will tell you it was Bill's infatuation with Simon's daughter that led to the murder; he'd sent her lewd notes and declared he couldn't live knowing he would *never* have her. Bill was on drugs, unstable, stealing. He was enraged. He sought revenge. The prosecution had endless plausible motives, but after recording hundreds of hours of interviews with Bill at Waikeria Prison, I remain unconvinced that he did it. I mean, it's possible, *anything is possible*, but is it irrefutable? There's no evidence of a temper, or poor impulse control, and don't get me started on the incompetency of his original defence.

Like all good and all bad things in Bill Ruatara's life, it was a matter of chance and circumstance. Fate conspired to place him in the path of the Primrose family. It's the worst thing that ever happened to him.

If you believe Bill's version of events, he simply found the bodies, heard the sirens and panicked, fleeing the crime scene. Wrong place, wrong time. Putting aside my own personal judgement, the case ultimately boils down to two facts:

One: Bill Ruatara has experienced lifelong severe asthma.

Two: Bill Ruatara did not have an inhaler on the night of the murders.

When he was on trial, the jury decided the second fact was a lie, or at least they seemed to believe a man with severe asthma was capable of running 2200 metres at near Olympic speed *without* an inhaler. Just minutes before the first screams were heard, he'd been captured on CCTV over two kilometres away. He couldn't have been in two places at once.

There were, of course, many other issues with the original trial, from the general reluctance of the police to investigate other potential suspects, to their coercive interview techniques with witnesses, including Bill. And the fact the police disposed of evidence immediately after Bill's conviction means it won't be available for the retrial – when we get there.

Bill didn't do himself, or his lawyers, any favours the morning of the murders; at approximately 6 am, Bill Ruatara walked 900 metres from his flat, past the ATM outside The Pope sports bar, past the strip of shops and the service station, to the Morning Star bakery on the corner of Pope Terrace. As he made his way there, he placed a shopping bag full of ashes into a skip beside the BP. The ashes were once the clothes he'd worn the night prior when he visited the Primrose house. At the bakery he sat and ate a mince and cheese pie, staring out into the quiet street. These facts alone don't make him a murderer, but they sure as shit didn't help his defence. It also didn't help that he cut his nails to the quick that morning, shaved his head, cleaned the flat he'd recently started renting with bleach and destroyed his mobile phone. People don't really understand what trauma, fatigue and drug-induced chemical imbalances in the brain can do to someone's behaviour.

The criminal justice system is a complex apparatus, contingent above all else on the principle that someone, anyone, is innocent until proven *guilty*. Not proven shifty, or strange, or even murderous. Just *guilty*. Behaving suspiciously after exposure to extreme violence, blood and entrails should not automatically get a man locked up for twenty-five years. Innocent or not, Bill Ruatara was never given a fair shake of it.

•

I indicate and pull into the road. I'm getting close now. I've been out here a few times over the years. It's rural, but not populated by the poor, struggling farmers you'd expect. Half the land is used to graze racehorses or ponies; the other half is used for dairy. The occupants of these big farm estates are all as rich as anyone you might find in an Auckland penthouse or the hidden bays of Waiheke Island. The Primrose family was no exception but, unlike the others around this part of the country, their money didn't come from horse racing or dairy farming.

The Primrose house is still beautiful, despite the horrors it has seen. Some locals wanted it torn down, others thought it needed to be burnt. According to property records, it was owned by the Primrose family trust, and they ultimately decided to leave it standing. Then five years ago it was purchased by a developer, who rebuffed my early attempts to get inside. He didn't want anyone reminded about the dark past of the property he was trying to sell. I suppose the house was cursed, because he ended up dividing the land, selling off most of the farmland and half the gardens. Then a year ago a family brought the house for a little over a million dollars, which is probably about a third of what it would be worth had it not been the site of one of New Zealand's most infamous crimes. The property is now owned by the De Koenings. Thus far, all attempts to contact the De Koenings have failed, and that's why I have driven down today.

My phone rings through the car speakers. It's Lynn.

I ignore it for now. My phone talks to me through the speakers.

'*Message from Lynn: "I know you're not working, and we need to talk. Your mum said you're going to Europe . . . were you going to run this by me? How do you plan on helping out with school fees and everything else without a job? Call me back, TK."*'

I exhale. She's busy, probably stressed about work, the new baby coming. I remember what it was like when Esther was born. The stress, prenatal classes, the uncertainty about how it will all happen. But then it just *happens* – howling, grunting, midwives with beatific smiles and kind eyes, the wet earth smell. The surge of emotion. We were both too charged with adrenaline to panic. When the contractions started at home, I set up an obstacle course around our living room to distract her, to keep her moving through those early hours of labour. *Seems like a lifetime ago*, I think as I turn onto Jacksons Road.

I expect the house is probably in better condition than the last time I was down here. I'd taken photos to show Bill; his idea, not mine. He was writing his memoir and wanted the photos to help him recall his time at the house. When I showed him the images taken from the gate, his brow creased.

'Gwen would lose her mind over the state of the gardens.'

*Gwen Primrose*: whip-smart matriarch, first-class finance graduate, never worked a day in her life. I was always most interested in her, psychologically. I feel for them all, given the horrible circumstances of their deaths, but Gwen's interior world and the life she lived with Simon fascinate me most. Was she ever happy? Did she know all of his secrets? How did she balance her love for her children with his betrayals and lies?

Now I pull up outside the iron gates. They attach on either side to a stone wall, the sort you might find in the British countryside, which runs along the width of the property. The drive curves up to the brow of a hill, lined with low-hanging trees. Last time I was here, you could barely see the house through the tall grass and unruly hedges. Now it's all neat and straight.

I reach out to press the intercom by the gate. I am about to find out if this two-hour drive was a waste of time or not. A woman's voice comes through the speaker.

'Hello?'

'Hi,' I say. 'My name's TK – ah, Te Kuru Phillips. I was just hoping to chat to you about the house. I work with Bi—'

'Leave us alone.' Each syllable is bitten off with such rage I can't get a word out before the hint of static from the speaker disappears and the conversation is over. I press the button once more.

'Did you not hear what I said? I *will* call the police if you don't clear off right now.'

'Look, it could help his case. Bill may be innocent. I just want to see inside—'

'No. Go away. We just want to live our lives.'

I stare up at the house, before reaching out and shifting the car in reverse. The last thing I notice before turning away is a man up in the bedroom window, looking down at me.

# TWO
## SLOANE

YOU REACH A moment during any good hangover when the idea of taking another sip of booze at last becomes palatable – not just palatable, desirable. I think back over the night, count the drinks off. Four champagnes, two chardonnays, one Ardbeg with a friend – the editor of the *Sydney Morning Herald* – and two glasses of water before bed, as if that'll undo the inevitable.

Last night was the very first *big* night I've had since things went south with Rain. I know, *Rain*. The name alone should have been a red flag. Early on in our relationship, Rain was very eager to establish *rules* about his wants and needs. He threw the word 'poly' around a lot; eventually I understood that this was a clever way to say he was still sleeping with other women. I ended up letting him walk all over me. Everyone wants to be good-looking because you really can get away with almost anything. Rain sure did. I still cringe thinking about the fact we lasted almost six months.

I hadn't expected to drink so much last night, but then again I hadn't expected to win. I was already a few glasses deep when the host – firebrand journalist Des Holder – read out my name. I'd looked around, checking the faces at my table to make sure I'd heard correctly. Everyone was grinning at me, then they'd got to their feet, clapping at me like trained seals.

'Me . . . I won?'

The rest of the night is a blur, but at least I managed to get through my acceptance speech without tears. I thanked my producer, my team, my assistant, Tara. I expressed deep sadness for the victims, along with hope that my podcast and book would help shine a light on domestic violence. I hope I didn't sound like an asshole, mouthing off platitudes and giving myself a pat on the back. It's not always easy to get the balance right when you're reporting on crimes.

I roll over, a wave of queasiness washing over me. I do miss having Rain here sometimes. The comfort of a warm body beside me, company for the awards. I stretch my limbs in the crisp hotel sheets, finding my phone. It's almost midday. I have the itch to open all the usual suspects, to start the social media treadmill – Instagram, Twitter, email, refresh each, do it all over again – but I've been off social media for a few months. We only have the podcast accounts now.

I skim through the emails on my phone, contemplating the idea of a greasy, room-service breakfast. *Do they do breakfast this late?* I have one more night in Sydney before heading back to Melbourne tomorrow morning. Despite being unwell lately, my assistant has checked and filtered my emails. She has also emailed me directly, flagging an article about a case in New Zealand.

I click the link and read.

It's oddly familiar. I may have read about it years earlier. A private chef stabbed each member of the family he had worked for. Now, seventeen years later, there are growing calls for a retrial. With seven years left of his sentence to serve, a confession or acknowledgement of guilt would likely make him eligible for parole. According to the article, that's out of the question. *Could be something?* Tara wrote in the subject line of her email. She's right. The next podcast? An article? A book perhaps? There's a lot of story here, lots to investigate. I close the link and open another email, this time from my producer, Esteban. He's got his own ideas. He wants me to look at the case of a family who disappeared without a trace in Adelaide in the late nineties. I close my laptop. Today is not a workday. Today is a recovery day. The next project can wait.

Reaching for the phone beside the bed, my body feels like cement slowly setting. I dial room service.

'Eggs benedict please, room 903. A double espresso. Oh and a Bloody Mary, if it's not too early.' I'm already at the critical point of booze palatability.

'Sure. Won't be too long.'

My throat feels as coarse as pine bark. I drag myself out of bed to the bathroom, dipping my head under the faucet like a dog. I turn back and see a note near the door. It's on white card. I pick it up, and as I read the hangover twists. I could be sick.

*YOU WILL PAY.*

I tear the door open and crane my head out, looking left then right in the hallway. The note could have been pushed under my door anytime through the night or the morning. *Who knows my room number?* Someone at the hotel, or someone else? I think about the emails I received in the past. I had a stalker for a few weeks when I was investigating, but I haven't heard from him in almost a year. Is he back?

# In My Defence

## Chapter One

Everyone knows how it ends: my chef's knife buried to the hilt in Simon's chest. My fingerprints all other the crime scene. My boot prints in the blood. That's where this story leads, but few people know where it truly begins.

A phone call. As simple as that. I wish I hadn't bothered getting up at all that day; otherwise I would have kept sleeping, I would have called back later, too late. My uncle might have already died, and maybe I'd have decided to stay in Australia. But that's not how life is, there is no *otherwise*.

It was five in the morning and I'd gotten home from work at one. The landline never rang that early, especially on a Sunday. I knew it was something. My housemate banged on the door, I forget his name but he didn't get much sleep either. A DJ, club rat, who dressed and acted like Iggy Pop.

'Someone's on the phone,' he said, his jaw going. It turned out he hadn't slept yet at all.

'Who?'

'She said she's your aunty. It's important.'

And it turned out it was. My uncle, the man who raised me after my mother died, had a heart attack in the night. He was on the third step of the staircase when his heart gave out. He'd clutched his chest, fallen back and hit his head. Now he was on life support. I didn't go back to sleep. I didn't think at all. I made a coffee, went to the travel agents and waited until it opened at 9 am, then I booked a flight from Melbourne back to Auckland that afternoon. I wept on the plane and drank four tiny bottles of Jim Beam with Diet Coke. I must have known in my bones I wasn't coming back to Melbourne: why else did I book one way? Why else did I take my chef's knives?

My uncle died sometime while I was soaring over the unbroken blue of the Tasman Sea. The funeral was three days later. By the time I called my boss on Thursday, he gave me twenty-four hours to get back. There were bills to pay for the funeral, to support my aunty. I helped with what little money I had saved.

In those first few days I spent most of my time with Maia. Grief is as effective as Cupid's arrow for bringing lovers back together. The familiarity of Maia's body was the ultimate comfort. We picked up where we left off when I moved to Australia. We'd just lie in bed for hours, talking.

'Do you remember how much we used to chat at school?' she asked.

'I was shy,' I said.

'You were. We'd hold hands at school, just walk around. It's weird to think about now. Pashing at the back of the rugby field.'

I laughed, pulling her closer.

'You were a lot chattier when you got home from school, on MSN.'

'That's where we first started chatting,' I said, casting back. I was there, six years ago, in the late nineties. Sitting on the one computer in the house, dialling into the internet.

'I know,' she said. 'I used to sign in and out until you noticed I was online. Hoping you'd chat.'

'I always did.'

'You always did.'

I was comfortable being back. Happy almost. But still ambitious. Word got out I was back in Rotorua and soon my other uncle, Mooks, got in touch. He was the one who first mentioned the Primrose family. He called me and said he just finished a gardening job for a rich family and they were looking for a private chef.

'It's a mansion, boy, and the pay is good.'

'I'm not a private chef,' I told him. 'And I won't be around for long.'

'They don't know that, do they?'

'Won't they want a resumé or a CV or something?'

'I'm tossing you a big juicy bone here, Bill. You decide if you want chew it. These people have more dollars than sense.'

After a few interviews at restaurants in town, I knew I wasn't going to make anything like the money I was on in Australia. Work was thin, and I'd be starting on half of what I got at Noir. I asked Uncle Mooks how I should apply.

He gave me an email address and before long I was on the bus to Cambridge. Mooks picked me up from the bus stop.

'I think it's for the best if they don't know we're related,' he said. 'I'll drop you at the gate and pick you up in half an hour.'

'Why?'

'They fired me. I don't hold grudges, but they didn't like how I tended the gardens. British, they're all funny about their plants, you know. I'm more about mowing lawns, pulling weeds.'

'They fired you?'

He just smiled. 'Don't worry about that. I got plenty of work lined up, starting at the high school soon. When you see the gardens they've got back there, you'll see what I mean. Too tricky for someone like me to keep on top of.'

He took me to a place with an iron gate and stone walls. I thought there might have been a castle inside, and I wasn't far off. The house was palatial, at least to me. Two storeys, four large bedrooms, living, dining, rumpus room, a pool room, an office, kitchen and a huge walk-in pantry. The kitchen was well equipped. You probably want to know about the knives. My knives. The ones used to stab each member of the family.

'Yes, hello. May I help you?' A woman's voice greeted me through the intercom. Not with the posh British accent I was expecting, but the long throaty consonants and puckered vowels of French.

'Hi, I'm, ah, here for the interview.'

'The chef, yes?'

'Ah, yeah, for the private chef role.'

'Okay, one moment please. I'll get the gate.'

There was a grinding sound as the huge gates began to swing inward.

'Drive up.'

But of course I didn't drive. I didn't have a car. Mooks was parked up across the road, so I walked all the way up the driveway to the front of the house. The great wooden door opened just as I raised my hand to the brass knocker. There, standing barely five feet tall, was Fleur. She was older than me – late twenties, dark hair, pale skin and fire-hydrant red lips. To be honest, I wasn't expecting the nanny to be wearing make-up, but that was Fleur – always looking her best.

'Well,' she said. 'No car?'

'No,' I said. 'Ah, I got a ride with a friend.'

She arched a perfectly manicured eyebrow, then led me inside. I couldn't keep my eyes off her. She had a magnetism. Something exotic and sophisticated. I followed her to the lounge area, startled by a taxidermic bear that loomed across the room. I remember thinking, *That's something you don't see every day*.

'Take a seat.'

I lowered myself into a leather Chesterfield. I instantly noticed something else – a white comb, encased in a glass box on the mantel. Three prongs, koru patterns etched into the side. I noticed other things too: art, hardwood furniture, other shows of opulence and wealth. I waited on the couch with my resumé and ambition bundled up in my lap. Fleur left me there. Then ten minutes later a door opened, and a much older woman came out.

'Bill?' she said.

'That's me.'

She reached out her hand. 'Pleasure to meet you. I'm Gwen Primrose.' In our correspondence, her full name appeared in her email signature: *Gwendolyn Bethany Primrose*. She gave a tiny nose-wrinkled smile. 'Come on through.'

She guided me to an expansive office overlooking the garden. The walls were lined with books. She sat down behind the desk.

'This is my husband's office, but I thought it would be the best place to talk. Official business, this.' She took a seat and smiled. 'So,' she said, glancing down at my resumé. 'You haven't worked as a private chef before.'

I swallowed. 'Umm. No. Most of my work has been for one of the top chefs in Melbourne. Noir was the only Australian restaurant ranked in the top one hundred in the world. It has three chef ha—'

'Is that so?' she said, cutting me off.

'Yes. And I've also helped a catering company to cater events.' I didn't mention it was for a marae up north, or that the *events* were tangi. I also didn't mention it was unpaid work when I was a teenager. I was making sandwiches.

'I can cook anything you like.'

'Anything?' she said.

I wanted to say I cooked for my family for years even before I became a chef. I wanted to tell her I was a lifelong student of the kitchen and was always seeking new recipes, trying new combinations of ingredients. But I couldn't summon the words to my mouth. I just found myself nodding. 'Yeah, I think so.'

'And, you are, ahh—' She moved her hand in front of her face. 'What's your heritage, Bill?'

'My heritage?'

'You're not white, what's your ethnicity?'

I felt heat at the back of my neck. 'Oh—' I should have asked why that was important, but I knew I wouldn't get the job if I pushed back. Her gaze narrowed. I felt like a bug pinned to a board. 'My dad, he was Māori. I mean, part Māori. So, yeah, I'm part Māori. Part English, and who knows whatever else.' I swung for humour and missed.

'Right.' She tilted her head. 'How *interesting*, so you must be all clued up with the local cuisine.'

'We don't have too much. We mostly inherited the British diet, I think.'

'There must be some things?'

*Pork bones and pūhā, fry bread, hāngi, kina.* All the clichés sprang to mind. 'Yeah, I suppose there are a few.'

'Well, I'd be eager to learn more.'

The interview continued. I tried my best to answer her questions, to make a good impression, but by the end it felt like she was going through the motions. It was as though she had already decided I wasn't going to get the job. Then she said, 'And you could live on site? It's important that you are available twenty-four hours. We've found it difficult to find someone who can commit to this, but we think the compensation is fair.'

I hadn't asked about the pay and was almost afraid to mention it.

'Yeah,' I said. 'That would work. I could live on site. And the compensation—'

'Ninety thousand dollars,' she said. 'Plus free rent and food.'

I realised my mouth had fallen open. I thought about Maia, but I knew this opportunity wouldn't come around again. Private chef experience would be great for future work, and the money was almost three times what I was offered in Rotorua. I already suspected I would have to live in Cambridge for the job; the commute would be a lot from Rotorua. The house, the luxury, was seductive to my twenty-one-year-old brain. It had an intoxicating effect. I was already imagining plush beds, soft sheets and a spacious room. 'That's perfect.'

'Great, so how soon would you be available?'

'Well, if I got the job, I could start straightaway.'

She rose. 'Why don't we start tomorrow?'

Was this a test? 'This tomorrow?' I said, and she laughed.

'You're a funny young man, Bill. Yes, *this* tomorrow.'

I had everything I needed. I would be able to collect my clothes and things overnight. I would have to learn the kitchen, sharpen my knives, buy food. I would be making more money than I'd ever dreamt of, and it was all starting the next day.

'Of course. What time?'

'Nine am,' she said. 'Don't be late.'

I nodded, thinking about the bus schedule from Rotorua. Maybe Mooks could drop me back. 'Nine am. Sure, thank you,' I said. Turning to leave, I glanced over the lawn toward the cottage and my eyes snagged on something. A young woman with her feet up on an outdoor table. She wore glasses and held a book in her hand.

'That's Elle, our daughter,' Gwen said, noticing my stare. 'I hope you can make a cracking salad. She's just decided she's a vegetarian now.' She rolled her eyes.

In the garden, Elle turned, lowered her glasses with her index finger and looked in at me. For the second time that day I felt snared by the gaze of a Primrose woman.

# THREE

## TK

OVER EIGHTY-FIVE PER cent of people think he's guilty as sin, according to a poll attached to a news story from last year. We'd been trying to get some media for the retrial campaign – something we thought would be a positive thing and build some momentum. It hadn't ended up being as simple as that. While I don't think the poll is necessarily a fair indication of public opinion – mostly crackpots vote in those things, after all – it does point to how hard it will be to find an impartial jury for a retrial. I think about it now as I sit across from Bill in the meeting room of the prison.

Bill's only a few years older than me. When he was arrested, I was only sixteen years old and about to embark on what would be six years of study. Forensic psychology. My parents were proud then, less so these days.

'Lawrence came by yesterday,' Bill says.

Lawrence is Bill's lawyer, mid-forties, a penchant for tie clips and social justice.

'What did he say?'

'He was optimistic about getting a retrial. Maybe he's just trying to keep my spirits up.'

Being wrongfully imprisoned for seventeen years gives someone every right to be cynical. The damage that kind of injustice does is hard to overstate: trust issues with authority, society, the legal system, of course. Everyone. I remind myself how privileged I am to be in the circle of people Bill trusts. Strange, given how few other people in my life trust me.

'Sometimes I wonder about him,' Bill says. 'What he really thinks. I reckon you're the only one who actually thinks there is a chance I'm innocent.'

He's not wrong. The media has not been kind. And there's more to come. Netflix has just announced a mini-series *based* on the Primrose massacre. Part of some local content push. *Based.* I wonder what the ending will be.

I debate in my mind whether I should divulge this information. In the end, I can't keep it from him.

'Netflix,' he says. 'That's TV?'

'Yeah. Apparently George Clooney is going to play you.'

The tension in his face disappears. 'You reckon?' A smile. 'Maybe if he was twenty years younger, you cheeky bastard.'

I laugh at that.

'Oh, someone got in touch,' he says. 'I told Lawrence about it, but he told me to ask you.'

'Ask me what? Who got in touch?'

'The assistant of some journalist in Australia. I don't know. Sloane someone. Weird name, I thought. Not many Kiwis named Sloane.'

'No,' I agreed, a prickle on my neck. *It can't be*, I think. 'Sloane Abbott?'

'Yeah,' Bill says, frowning. 'That's the one. Sloane Abbott. Her assistant sent me a letter, then called. Asked if I would be interested in talking to Sloane.'

*This is big*, I think. If Bill is the subject of her next podcast, it means huge exposure, a deep dive on the facts. She will expose all the shortcomings of the investigation and the defence. 'Sloane Abbott just got a historical rape trial to court in Australia. She's the sort of woman you want on your side, Bill.'

Another long pause. He's staring at his hands, unreadable. Injustice hits people in the gut when they can see themselves in the victim, and that's the problem here. Like so many men in this country, Bill is trapped by some hidden code of masculinity, of pride: he doesn't externalise his emotions, he doesn't speak out about those who have wronged him in the past; the most he's opened up is in his manuscript. People don't empathise with Bill because they can't read him. They also can't comprehend his behaviour after the crime, when he seemed to act unhinged. What they don't realise is that viewed through a psychoanalytical lens, Bill's behaviour was not so abnormal. But people hear that he burnt his clothes, that he shaved his head and they see guilt. The truth is: no-one knows how they would react. People like Bill, who look like Bill, are also conditioned to fear the police, to be wary of authority. He was arrested and had his wrist broken by a cop when he was sixteen for the terrible crimes of underage drinking and breaching a liquor ban. The night Bill discovered the bodies, he would have panicked. Gone into a strange mix of fight and flight response.

'But I don't know her. I can't trust her,' he says now.

The last time Bill spoke to a podcast for an episode, another naïve idea that we lived to regret, they did nothing to help him appear innocent. In fact, they added fuel to the fire. It was more of an attack than journalism.

'I won't tell you what to do, Bill. I don't know her either, don't know if she is trustworthy, but she's effective. I'll give her that.'

'What if she just wants a story? What if she doesn't want to help?'

'I can talk to her first?' I offer. 'Feel her out.' A podcast can be produced and put out fast, unlike a book. It can be published in weeks, or even days. And potentially has wider reach than traditional media, is global. I can feel myself getting excited about what Sloane's interest could mean for us, for Bill.

But he looks dubious. The foreign press was particularly harsh on Bill, especially the tabloids in the UK, who paid big money for interviews with former teachers, ex-girlfriends, Gwen's aunt Lizzie – anyone who'd ever had a grudge against him or were prepared to invent one for their five seconds of fame. The public outrage reached fever pitch as the trial ramped up and more details of the murders emerged. But if we could make sure Sloane got the facts . . .

'Can I ask you something, TK?' Bill says, breaking my train of thought.

'Of course.'

'Why do you still come here?'

'What do you mean? I come to help.'

'But you don't see other inmates. You don't have the lanyard. You're not working anymore, right?'

I cringe. I think about my fridge door, the magnetic peg that holds the bills, the march of mortgage repayments. I see the post-card too, from somewhere in Portugal, nothing but my name and address written on the back. I imagine leaving, but then I think about Esther, my daughter.

'Well, I'm your friend.'

'What happened? How come you stopped working?'

I cut my eyes to the door. Could he know more than he is leading on?

'I quit,' I say. 'A couple of years ago. But I wanted to continue seeing you, helping you.'

Two years without work. It's amazing how far you can stretch some savings if you live simply. The cash pile won't last forever, though.

'Why?'

'I believe you, Bill. That's why. And knowing you're rotting away in here when you should be living your life outside, that's what brings me back every week.'

He seems to accept this without any further comment.

'Give her my book,' he says eventually. He is talking about the manuscript he's written. 'If she reads it and wants to talk to me, and you think it's for the best . . . well, then she can come visit.'

'Good,' I say. 'I'm going away next week, so it would be good for you to have someone else to bother you while I'm away.'

'Where you going? Holiday?'

'Something like that,' I say. 'I thought I mentioned it.'

He smiles. 'You did, but you didn't say where you were off to.'

'You won't like it,' I say. 'So I'm going to keep it to myself.'

His smile falters. 'TK, tell me. I want to know.'

'I'm visiting Fleur, in France, and, ah, I might track down Tate . . .' I hesitate, watching as the lines between his eyes, beside his mouth, deepen. The family have all moved on, justice served, so she doesn't know I'm coming. But I know she can help, even if she hates Bill, even if she wants nothing to do with him or me or anyone else. 'And Elizabeth,' I say.

'Elizabeth . . .'

'Primrose.'

Bill stands suddenly, eyes fierce. 'No,' he says. 'They won't help. *She* won't help. She is half the reason I'm here.' He rubs at the sides of his head, his voice is louder now. 'Everyone believes I'm the killer, and she will make you believe that too.' He turns and strides away.

'Bill, listen—'

The guard opens the door, and Bill disappears through it. His bowed head and hunched shoulders are the last thing I see before the door slams shut.

# FOUR

## SLOANE

TARA'S BEEN IN contact with the lawyer of the convicted murderer from the 2005 Primrose stabbings and she's sent through a couple more recent articles. I've been thinking about it a lot – working on something new helps me forget about the potential stalker – so it feels like fate when I hear from Bill Ruatara's psychologist, Te Kuru Phillips. I forward the message to Tara, who immediately calls me.

'What do you think?'

'I think you should go and speak with him,' she says. 'It's such a juicy case.'

'Maybe,' I say. 'And what's your opinion on Bill Ruatara?'

'*Ruatara*,' she corrects with stronger, continental vowels, rolling both r's. 'Not guilty,' she says. 'Absolutely not guilty, but the world thinks he is. There's been petitions and groundswell support for a retrial. And reading over the facts of the case, there's definitely more to the story here.' She would know. Tara moved over from New Zealand as a kid; she always has one eye on what is happening in her birth country.

Bill's psychologist has a proposal. I can do a podcast on the Primrose stabbings, but he has two requests, which in this context sound like a euphemism for rules: I can't release any episodes until he's listened to the entire season first. Harsh, but potentially fair. The second is he wants to meet with me before I interview Bill Ruatara and make sure I have the best intentions. It's all a bit presumptuous. I believe myself to be impartial: one must keep an arm's distance from the subject, that's a core tenet of good investigative journalism.

There's something else that the psychologist mentioned: Bill Ruatara has written a book in prison, and apparently it's pretty good. His side of the story. He's looking for a publisher and thought I might be able to put him in touch with someone. It's possible, I suppose, but most publishers won't want to touch it, unless he's proven innocent. Then it would be hot property. Assuming the Proceeds of Crime Act is the same in New Zealand as it is in Australia, a publisher would have no incentive to publish it, as no-one would be permitted to make money off his retelling of a crime for which he's been convicted. Extra motivation, I suppose, for him to have his conviction overturned.

There's always a tingling sensation in my chest when I stumble upon something I know has heat, has urgency, when something is humming with story potential.

I go to Twitter for a temperature check. I might be the only journalist in the world not addicted to it, and the only reason we have an account is for the podcast, and to post updates on coming projects. Tara manages it, but she shares my social media allergy – she got rid of her personal accounts a while back too – perhaps that's why we get on so well. We both share a philosophy: anything that is that addictive, and can affect your mood that much, is not positive.

But there's more to it for me. I'd found I was viewing the world through the lens of social media, rather than living in the moment. When I found myself assessing the my day-to-day life for its content potential, I knew it was time to stop. So I killed my personal accounts and restricted my use to work-related stuff only – my podcast had to have an online presence, of course, and I need to be able to access sites like Twitter and Reddit for research. Now it is just another source to me, nothing more.

On Twitter, a couple of cursory searches yield only further unanswered questions to go with all the others that surround this case. It had captured the attention of the world for fifteen minutes. According to the psychologist, there are one or two key pieces of evidence that would overturn Ruatara's conviction. Te Kuru Phillips – or TK, as he signed his email off – quit his job two years ago and has committed his life to justice . . . that in itself is a story.

If I need any more incentive to pursue this, it comes in the form of late-night hate mail. My skin crawls. This is why I almost never check the tip line emails myself; so much misogyny, so many creeps and possible stalkers. If I hadn't checked my emails, I never would have seen it; Tara would have screened it. This begs the question: how many others like this has she screened in the past? The message is in the subject line, that's how they do it. That way you don't need to open the email to see what they have to say. *SEE YOU SOON.*

I click. That's it. The image that makes me book flights to New Zealand. When you make a podcast about a famous athlete and their potential involvement in a historical murder of an ex-partner, all sorts of men's rights activists, overzealous sports fans and general creeps crawl out of the woodwork to enlighten you with all the ways they would like to see you die. But this one counts as a genuine threat. I am looking at a series of images taken of me. They are from yesterday, taken from the co-working space we work in. Then from my walk home to my apartment. Then an image from behind me as I open my door.

I think about the note in my hotel room again. The threats are cheesy, unoriginal. But, still, I don't like to take chances with potential psychopaths. I don't tell Tara, as she's supposed to be on leave, but I do contact a friend in the police, forwarding the message on.

I'll go to New Zealand, meet TK, the psychologist, and if nothing comes of it, I'll take myself skiing in Queenstown. In spite of every feminist impulse in my body, I message Rain. I tell myself this will be the last time.

*Busy?*

He arrives sometime after five and instantly I feel better. I know I'm using him, a man, to feel secure and protected, and I shouldn't have to, but this is the world we live in. If you have a profile, and you choose to put yourself out there, this is what happens. It happens to everyone from Rihanna to Sanna Marin, to little old me. Okay, not *everyone*. Women who do something that upsets men.

When Rain slides into bed and kisses me, I kiss him back. I pull his hard body against mine and he reaches around, squeezing me. God, he's a good kisser. He drags my body on to his and I slide down, unbuckling his jeans.

'I missed you,' he says.

I look up at him. I forget the message, the stalker, the morning flight. I just focus on him. 'I missed you too.' A tiny lie, but it's the least I can do.

## In My Defence

### Chapter Two

When I told Maia about the job, she was surprised at how quickly I was moving in with strangers. We'd fallen into a comfortable routine. I'd help out with my aunty in the evening in Rotorua before heading to Maia's for the night. She was living at her brother Michael's flat, in a rough part of town. It was a little like we were in high school again: self-conscious, learning each other's bodies. We were charged with the excitement of a second chance and made up for lost time with our voracious appetites for each other.

'So you're just going to stay there with them? Live in Cambridge?'

'Yeah, I guess. Free rent.' I tried to make a joke of it, but she didn't smile. 'I'll save up for a couple of weeks and get a cheap car so I can come and go.'

'And I can visit you there too.'

I knew it wasn't a question but I answered. 'I'll check.'

'What do you mean?'

'I don't know their rules. I bet it's fine.'

We hadn't had the awkward talk yet. I'd decided she was my girlfriend again, but we hadn't put a label on it. When I went to Melbourne she stayed on for her last year of high school. She wanted to be on TV, a news presenter, but I'd told her they never had people like us on the news – never reporting it, anyway. But still, she had her dreams and they didn't involve Melbourne. With her thick Kiwi accent, she was certain the only place for TV opportunities was New Zealand.

•

The Primroses all had their nicknames. Gwendoline was *Darling* to her husband, *Mummy* to the kids and *Gwen* to everyone else. Mr Primrose was *Si* to his wife, *Dad* to Elle and Chet, and *Simon* to all of the staff. Chet was *Chester William Simon Primrose* when he was in trouble. Elle was always just *Elle* – she was never in enough trouble to get her full name. Parents aren't supposed to have favourites, but it was clear how much love and attention the firstborn got in that family.

They were all gathered in the living room when I arrived with my tattered suitcase. I'd worn the same clothes again, my only good shirt and tidy jeans, trying to look the part. I would be able to wear my chef's whites once I was working.

'Bill, hello,' Gwen said. 'Put your bag down here, we can sort that out after you meet the family.'

The scene felt oddly staged. Simon sat in the deep Chesterfield armchair. Elle and Chet sat with a wide gap between them on the three-seater. Chet was positioned deep against the leather back of the seat, legs straight so his feet were off the floor. Elle sat forward, her legs crossed at the shin, chin in palm, head askew. Her blue eyes were fixed on me. Gwen perched on the arm of the couch with her legs twined together. So naturally elegant, both women, while the men felt artificially placed. They could have been models, posed for a photoshoot. Fleur was at the table folding clothes.

A gust of wind at my back gave me the impression the house was inhaling, sucking me in.

'Well, come on,' Gwen said. 'Close that door, the fire is going.'

I stepped in and pulled the living room door shut. I left my suitcase by the door.

'Hi,' I said.

Simon stood, came over. He stretched out his hand. I was expecting a plummy posh accent like hers, but his was different. Harsher, thicker somehow.

'Alright, Bill. Pleasure to meet you. I hear you know your way around a kitchen.'

I smiled. 'I like to think so.'

'Well, you charmed my wife, no mean feat. Took me a number of years, in fact.'. A soft jab on my arm. 'This is Chet, my son.'

Chet stared for a moment, before pulling himself up and offering his hand.

'And my daughter,' he added.

'Elle,' she said, rising. She was liquid, with a warm smile. 'It's nice to meet you, Bill. Mummy has told me all about you.'

'Well, I'm just looking forward to cooking you people some good food.'

Simon's smile broadened. *'You people* - I like him already. Such a strong working-class Kiwi accent, isn't it?'

'So,' Gwen interjected, 'Bill is going to be living in the cottage with Fleur and cooking for us, just how Marlon did back home. You can ask him to make you anything.'

'Can he make Marlon's poutine?' Chet asked, turning to his mum.

'Well, you may need to ask Bill that, he's right there.'

'I can do that,' I said, trying to smile. 'Sure thing. I don't know who Marlon is, but I make a mean poutine myself.'

Chet was quite pale, but a glow climbed up his cheeks. He couldn't meet my eye.

•

Any hope I had of a cushy, spacious room evaporated when I got to the cottage I was to share with Fleur. The only characteristic it shared with the house was a general feeling it had been there for a long time. Where the house had heritage features – ceiling roses, a pressed-tin roof, hardwood floors – the cottage had spiderwebs, threadbare carpet, and draughty sash windows. The main house had a kitchen the size of a large apartment, but the cottage kitchenette had a single stove, a toaster, kettle and a microwave. It felt like a converted stable, and it turned out that wasn't far off. It was once the milker's cottage. The original stables still stood out in the paddocks beyond the trees at the edge of the gardens. At first I was self-conscious sharing a bathroom with Fleur, but we got past that soon enough.

I put my suitcase down in my room and came out into the small dining and living area with its tiny box TV and old couch. 'This is our little honeymoon suite,' she said, her French accent sweetened with a hint of sarcasm. I turned to see her standing in the door frame of her room. 'Do you have a girlfriend?'

I was struck by how direct the question was. 'Yeah,' I said. 'Sort of.'

'Well, they don't like us to bring guests to the cottage. So perhaps it's best you don't bring her here. You can see her when you take breaks.'

'Oh, uh, thanks for the heads-up.'

'They are funny like that. But you get used to it. I think it's the British. They have their little habits, prudish. Is that the right word?'

'Well, it depends what you mean.'

She ignored me, turning back into her room. 'It gets cold out here. I have a heater in my room, you should get one too,' she called.

Then she closed the door.

# FIVE
## TK

I GO TO the fridge, eye the postcard, the bills. My stomach squeezes. I throw the door open, lurch forward, searching for a moment before realising there's only non-alcoholic beer in here. It's all automatic, like I'm just watching myself open the cupboard above the fridge, where once there were countless bottles of aperitifs, whisky, vodka, gin. Now there's nothing but the manual for my stove and an empty glass decanter collecting dust. Turning back, leaning against the fridge, I lower myself gently to the cold tiles of the kitchen floor. The bills. Internet, power, phone. After I pay them, pay the next couple of months' mortgage and for my trip, I'll not have much left at all. I'll have a master's degree, but no job.

As a psychologist, I was making good money. Then it ended. The rot started a few years ago when my marriage fell apart. Then I lost my brother. I managed to get by, managed to hide my drinking, my partying. For an entire year, I barely saw my daughter, thinking it wouldn't be healthy for her to see me go through all that, but I was always thinking about her. I was wrong to stay away from her. Esther fills the hole that was blown wide open inside of me; she was the only thing that could bring me back.

But now I sit here, anticipating the time when I won't be able to pay my bills. When I will have to sell, find a new job, move from the city and see my daughter even less.

I take my phone; I need to get back to Lynn. I inhale as deep as I can while the phone rings.

'TK,' she says. 'It's late.'

'Sorry,' I say. 'It's been a busy week.'

'Sounds like it.' A beat of silence. 'You're going away.'

'Just for a few days, less than a week.'

A long pause. 'When?'

'Next Friday.'

She clears her throat. I can feel her anger, like heat radiating through the phone. She manages to temper it when she speaks. 'Is that so? Where to?'

'Edinburgh, London, France.'

'Edinburgh. Right. Then London and France. Sounds lovely. Well, Esther will enjoy a trip away.'

She's being facetious. 'You know I'm not taking her, I can barely afford to take myself.'

'Well, this baby could come at any moment, you realise that? We can't have her on your days. We have appointments.'

'I'll sort something out.'

She scoffs. 'And you won't tell me what is so important? Why you're taking this little holiday now?'

'It's not a holiday,' I say. 'And no, I can't say.'

'Why not?'

'Because I'm not so sure myself.'

'Right, sure. It's all about TK.'

I don't have a response for that. I feel pressure at the back of my eyes. Pinching my forehead, I speak again. 'Look, I'm sorry, okay, Lynn? I'm getting better, I'm still working on myself, and this trip, it's going to help.'

She doesn't respond.

'You know I love that girl more than anything in the world. It's not all about me.'

'What about me? I'm thirty-eight weeks pregnant, TK. I could go into labour tonight.'

'I care about you, I do.' It's true. She's a good woman, and I nearly ruined her life. 'But . . . I loved her too, Lynn.'

Now I'm talking about Aroha and the room feels suddenly cold.

'No,' she says. 'We're not having that conversation now. I'll drop Esther off on Friday night. You better see her before your big trip.' Then the line dies.

After the call I search for Sloane online. She has a made-for-podcast husky voice, and when I finally see photos of her from the news articles, I find she has the looks to match. Blonde hair, cherub cheeks and bright smiling eyes.

I message her. *See you tomorrow, let me know if there are any issues.*

She gets back to me instantly. *Will do. Looking forward to it.*

I get why people like her. She refuses to publish the scintillating and salacious details of homicides – particularly domestic abuse cases – if it's not in the public's interest to know. So last year, when a woman was stabbed thirty times and disfigured by her former partner, Sloane's article simply stated: *The perpetrator murdered his ex-partner in the most horrendous circumstances, the details of which I refuse to publish here. The judge and jury will endure the gory details and deliver their verdict, but what's important for us to understand is how this man who had a DVO against him, and was banned from contact with his ex-partner, still managed to find her. This is just another failure by the justice system to protect a woman who fled an abusive environment.*

A journalist with a social conscience. I guess that's a little like a vegetarian shark. And yet she still manages to find enough in her stories to sustain a career. It makes me wonder about her approach to the podcast. And a guilty thought slides into my mind. *What if she does what I couldn't? What if she finds something I missed? What if she's the hero Bill needs?*

•

Sloane is somewhere over the Tasman when I eventually get out of bed the next day at around 9 am. I'm gnawing on all the information from the trial, what I know now, anticipating her questions. I assume she has read up on the case and knows the usual talking points.

*Why were his footprints all around the house after stepping in blood? Didn't he run straightaway? Why did he go to the house in the first place? Why did he change his story?*

There were other inconsistencies of course. The method and timing suggested a planned attack, but the prosecution proposed it was a crime of passion, a man suddenly snapping, killing without mercy or premeditation. There was the simple matter of timing too. The first screams were heard by the neighbours at 1.19 am. Phone records show the neighbours called the house three times: 1.19.25 am, immediately after the first scream, then at 1.21 am, and again at 1.24 am. After all three calls rang out, they called the police.

Meanwhile, Bill was captured on CCTV on the main street at 1.14.09 am, 2200 metres away. Bill had no car, and the world record 2000-metre run for men is 4.44.79. In order to be there at the time of the first scream, Bill would have had to cover 2200 metres in under six minutes. He was drunk, wearing jeans, skate shoes and a jumper. It's technically possible he ran, climbed the stairs and commenced the massacre, but highly unlikely. Especially when you consider the fact that he wasn't running in the footage that captured him passing the ATM, so he would have had to wait until he was just outside of the frame to start sprinting.

The prosecution offered a number of explanations for this. Errors in the timestamp of the CCTV, or on the phone records.

They suggested the first scream was possibly unrelated – the most viable of all their theories – or that something else woke Marie Gibbons next door and she had dreamt the scream. The other theories included the idea of an accomplice who picked Bill up and dropped him off, or a taxi, or even a stolen skateboard or bike – neither of which were recovered in extensive searches by the police. It's not uncommon in a legal defence to present a number of alternative theories to put doubt in the jury's mind, but it was a bold gambit for the prosecution. They didn't attach themselves to one theory, they just aimed to prove it was *possible*.

# SIX
## SLOANE

COMING THROUGH THE final stage of security screening, I see him waiting. He's hard to miss – he must be six foot three, at least.

'TK?' I say when I get to him.

'That's me,' he says. *Ah shit*, I think, *dimples, dark eyes*, my kryptonite.

'You're tall.'

'I'm tall,' he says. I was prepared to be a little intimidated given what I know about him, but somehow I'm not. He looks tired, but he's in good shape and there's no doubting he is handsome. I'd seen photos of him online, a profile from a few years ago. A child prodigy, apparently, earning early entry to university in Dunedin.

'How was your flight?'

'They thought it would be a good idea to sit me in a cluster of babies. So that happened.' I laugh. 'But I had my little pill and things weren't so bad.'

'You're a bad flyer?'

'Oh, terrible,' I say. 'The only thing keeping that plane in the sky is my mind.'

His eyes crease as he laughs. 'I feel that. Well, welcome to Aotearoa, anyway.'

'Pleasure to be here. Thanks for picking me up. Always nice to see a friendly face when you land somewhere new.'

'Well, I'm at your beck and call, just let me know if you need anything while you're here,' he says, leading me out through sliding doors into the cool Auckland air. 'It feels like I already know you so well. Because of the podcast, I guess.'

'People do say that, yeah. '

'Well, I am a huge admirer of yours – you do great work.' I could blush. 'Oh, thanks, that's nice of you to say.'

I've only brought a carry-on suitcase with me, so we head straight for the exit and across the road into a car park.

'This is me here,' he says, pointing at a four-wheel-drive.

'You know you can tell a lot about someone based on what car they drive.'

'Is that right?' There's a teasing note in his voice. 'And what does my 2005 Nissan Patrol tell you about me?'

'Well, you're a forensic psychologist. Successful, based on my Google searches. By all accounts extraordinarily clever. And yet this car would cost about four thousand dollars in Australia, probably the same here.'

'Go on.' He seems entertained.

'So you are either a really good saver who doesn't think it's worth spending money on a car, and don't mind the carbon output . . .'

'Or?'

'Or maybe you want to signal to someone, anyone, that you're not *really* materialistic. You go camping and hiking on the weekends, so you need a bit of power. And you're nostalgic for a slightly simpler time,' I say.

'Is that your professional psychological diagnosis of me?' There's laughter in his voice. 'Either a scrooge or some off-the-grid neo-luddite?'

'Am I wrong?'

'What if I told you my M Series was in the shop?'

'I wouldn't believe you. Not the type for luxury cars either.'

He opens the boot and pops my case in. I climb in the front, pull my belt across.

'I'm probably not as clever as you think, by the way. I just did well at school.'

'A prodigy, a genius, that's what I heard.' Now I'm teasing.

'I was a good problem-solver, that's all. Fluid intelligence peaks in our twenties and then continues to fade until we die.'

'What does that mean?'

'It means crystalised intelligence, or book smarts, is more important in old age. Experience and information are what we retain, but the problem-solving I was so great at is in a steep decline.'

'Is that true?' I say, fascinated. 'You are the most clever you will ever be in your twenties?'

'Short-term memory, quick thinking and pattern recognition all peak in late adolescence to mid-twenties.'

'I mean, it makes sense. The masterpieces, the brilliant world-changing businesses, all these things seem to happen for people in their twenties. How old are you?'

'Thirty-three,' he says.

'Your brain is basically stewed apple by this stage.' I'm taken by how quickly we've slipped into easy banter.

'So what does that mean at thirty-four?'

'Hey,' I say. 'You're not supposed to know that. Or say that.'

He smiles, shifting the car into reverse. 'Anyway, I crashed my Audi, wrote it off. Bought this one. It's the same car my dad used to drive. He's a fisherman. Hated the city. Raced horses. Still owns a few on his farm.'

'What did your mum do?'

'Nurse, then she had us. My sister and me and my twin.'

'You're a twin? That wasn't on your bio.'

'Was,' he says.

'Was?'

'I was a twin.'

'Oh, I'm sorry to hear.'

He sets out toward my hotel wearing a slightly sad smile. 'We lost him a few years back.'

In My Defence

Chapter Three


I was on a trial period for the first three months. I thought
even if I only lasted *that* long, just three months, and I
saved every dollar, I'd be well set up. I could travel the
world. Almost twenty-five thousand dollars, enough for a
house deposit. That was the first thing I thought: *Just make
it through the first few months*. How hard could that be?

They didn't want to tell me what they wanted for dinner,
they just wanted me to decide and have it ready on the table.
I went with a classic the first night: a lamb roast, with
crunchy potatoes, roasted kūmara, buttery peas and rich
gravy. Elle, being vegetarian, could only eat the vegetables,
so I thought a side salad with grains, pulses and grilled
artichoke would work. I'd cooked it all so many times before,

but still I was a little nervous, considering it wasn't as easy to find good fresh ingredients in Cambridge as it was in Melbourne.

I knew the kitchen, how to cook and plate, but I quickly realised my responsibilities went well beyond that. I was to buy ingredients from the local organic grocers and butchers each week. It was also my responsibility to serve and clean. Between meal-planning, shopping, cooking, serving and cleaning, I also had to prep lunches for Simon to take to work and for the kids to take to school. The kitchen was to remain spotless. I learnt all of this very quickly, but my first lesson on that first night was that I had to cook to a strict schedule. Seven pm sharp. Never a minute earlier or later.

The Primroses were seated at the table, the cutlery set. Gwen with a glass of white wine in front of her. The rest with water. I used the steel catering trolley from the walk-in pantry to freight the dishes to the table.

'Bon appétit.'

'Smells delicious,' Gwen said as I left the room.

From the kitchen I could see only her. I knew her eyes were on her husband, watching with anticipation. Then, when he murmured, 'Mmm, the lamb is tender,' she gave a small smile and started on her own meal, taking her knife and fork in her hands.

Later, Simon came to me in the kitchen as I started on the dishes. 'The gravy,' he said. 'It was a little salty. Otherwise, it was all very nice. Well done, you'll do just fine.'

'Thank you.'

Then they all went on with their evenings. That was it, the nerves disappeared and I realised I could do it. Everyone likes to eat good food, and the rich like good food most of all. What else do they have?

I'd drive the family car, the Range Rover, when I bought groceries – unless it was something small like butter or a loaf of bread, then I'd take my skateboard down the hills into the village. It was just a couple of kilometres, and at the end of our road was a footpath I could skate on. Gwen gave me a bank card to use for the shopping, and there was always a little cash available to take with me, but I never spent it on anything other than their food.

Fleur's au pair duties involved babysitting, helping with homework, washing and general tidying. She was almost like a fifth family member. She would sit and watch the news with the Primroses, and she would often eat lunch with Gwen when the kids were at school. She was a different person with them, proper and polished. *Warm.* Out in our cottage she wasn't cold or unkind, she was just more normal. She'd burp and laugh. She still wore her perfectly applied face of make-up, but she let herself be more comfortable out there.

One night, when the family had gone to bed and I was cooking myself a snack in the cottage, she came into the living area with a bottle of wine. It's clear she'd already had a couple of glasses.

'So, you drink?'

'Oh yeah,' I said.

'Not since you arrived. I noticed.'

'I'm trying to make a good impression, I suppose.'

'On them?' she laughed, took a sip of her wine from the mug she was using. 'I think you are okay. They don't mind too many drinks themselves, in case you had not noticed.'

I didn't go as far as saying so, but I had noticed – of course I had. Every night a few glasses of wine each. I just mumbled my agreement.

'Even the girl.'

'Elle?'

'I once bought her vodka to drink with her friends, back in the UK. They all put on an act, though.'

'Everyone here does?'

'What does this mean? *Everyone here.*'

'You seem a different person around me than you do around them.'

'Observant, aren't you? I play my part. But they play their roles almost every hour of every day. It's different. I'm working. It's expected. I am a good little au pair. You're a good little chef. No different.'

Fleur came closer. Reached past me, so close I could smell her perfume. She took another mug from the shelf, filled it and put it on the bench beside me.

'Don't be shy.'

I took a sip. I wasn't much of a wine drinker, and I didn't like the taste, but I drank it all the same. I sat down with my steak, fried egg and mashed potato, and I ate and drank. She watched me eat, talking.

'I moved with them, you know? That's why I act. I am repaying them for everything . . . I can't just leave, can I?'

'You want to leave?'

She rolled her tongue over her top lip.

'They wouldn't like that. They decide who comes and goes.'

I laughed but she just lifted her glass to her lips and took another drink.

'It gets a little lonely working over the other side of the world,' she said.

I felt my cheeks flush. She continued speaking.

'They don't like me to date, or to meet men, because they don't want strangers back at the house. I figure I can catch up on that when I finish, so I make do for now.'

'You can do what you want when you're not working?'

'I'm always working.'

'Not now.'

'No,' she said. 'I suppose. But even when we're not working, we always have to be available.' *We*, I noted. She was including me in this. 'If you let them down, it doesn't end well. I've seen it.'

Deliberate or not, her foot touched mine beneath the table. Just a passing glance as she recrossed her legs.

She drained the last of her wine. 'I met someone in London, a younger man. We keep in touch, but nothing will ever come of it. Not while I'm working for them.' Then she stood and went to bed.

•

Later that week, Elle watched me cook. We'd not had much interaction alone up until that point. Simon wanted stewed rabbit for dinner, a dish he'd had as a child visiting his great uncle's farm, so I'd organised it. I was cutting potatoes to go in the stew and Elle was sitting on the kitchen bench, her legs crossed beneath her.

'So, what do you do with the wine?'

'I just put a little in the sauce, it adds flavour.'

'But my brother can't drink.'

'Oh, I thought it would be fun to get him drunk.'

She snorted as she laughed and covered her mouth. 'Not funny, my dad would kill you.'

'The wine reduces and the alcohol boils out. So it's not really alcoholic by the time you eat. We'll have to find another way to get him liquored up.'

'I didn't expect you to encourage underage drinking,' she said, teasing.

I smiled, not turning away from the task at hand. I took the carrots and began to julienne them.

'Everyone my age drinks, you know. Our parents think we don't, but we do.'

'I was your age not so long ago, I know how it is,' I said.

'When did you start drinking?'

'I was probably twelve,' I say.

Her mouth opens. 'Really?'

'Yeah. Twelve, thirteen, we would pinch beers from my uncle or my friends' parents. Had my stomach pumped when I was fourteen after I got hold of a bottle of Jim Beam.'

'Wow,' she said.

'Do you miss it? London?'

'Like crazy,' she said. 'I wish I could click my fingers and move back.'

'Miss your friends, huh?'

'I'm making friends here at school, but not many. I do miss my old friends, my old life.'

'Yeah, it must be hard. Do you still keep in touch with them?'

'Not really. It's the middle of the night over there when we are awake. I can't just call. I try to chat on Messenger, and I can email. But they're all going on with their lives, I guess . . . I miss my boyfriend too.' She said it like an afterthought, like she wanted me to know. 'I guess he's my ex-boyfriend now.'

A long silence. I didn't know how to fill it, so I changed the topic. 'How long have you been vegetarian?'

'A few months,' she said. 'Dad didn't like it, *doesn't* like it. He's always making jokes that it's a phase, or that I'll end up anaemic. But I think it's important.'

'What made you go that way, then?'

'I just thought it was cruel, to kill animals. I like animals. We had a cat and a dog in London. The cat stayed there and the dog died not long before we left. I thought, why eat cows when we wouldn't eat our dog?'

I didn't feel like attacking her logic or airing my own opinions.

'No-one actually kills the animals themselves, that's why,' she said, answering her own question.

'Some do.'

'Butchers?'

'I killed them,' I said, nodding at the skinned rabbits on the chopping board.

'You did?' She said it as if heartbroken.

'They're a pest, introduced by settlers. I went out to a friend's farm. Your dad wanted rabbit and they're hard to buy at stores. I used to hunt pigs too, wild boar.'

Her eyes narrowed a little, not quite with disgust but something close.

'How do you hunt pigs? Aren't they tame?'

'Wild pigs. It's a bit of a New Zealand pastime. With dogs, out in the bush. Bit of fun and good eating.'

She rose and went to the rabbit. She prodded the flesh, salmon-pink with a tight sheen of pale fat.

'Is it easy?' she said.

'What? Hunting?'

'No.' She took the hind leg of a rabbit between her fingers with the detachment of a kid in science class. 'Is it easy to kill them? Do you feel bad?'

I turned and eyed her. *Weird girl*, I thought. 'It's easy enough. It just takes a few seconds, then it's over.'

'With a gun? Is that how you do it?'

'That's how I got the rabbits. With pigs, it's a knife.'

She swallowed. 'You stab them?'

'Can do. Or slit their throats. It's more humane, faster. You know?'

She looked like she might be sick. 'Makes sense.' Then she left the kitchen.

That night she wasn't at the table for dinner.

'Elle's feeling unwell,' Gwen told me.

'I'll put her dinner in the oven. If she's feeling better later, she can have it then.'

After dinner, the landline in the cottage rang. It was Gwen calling and when I heard her voice, I was certain I was in trouble. All the talk of drinking alcohol as a teenager and killing animals – it wasn't my smartest move. But I was wrong. She called to tell me Elle was feeling better and wanted a cheese-and-tomato toasted sandwich for dinner. I headed to the house to start cooking.

# SEVEN

## TK

SLOANE MEETS ME at the restaurant a few hours after I dropped her at the hotel. She's waiting at a small table in the corner under a muted bulb, a glass of white wine set beside the laptop she's typing away on. She takes her glasses off and stands. 'Hello again,' she says, with a smile.

'Good evening.'

'Let me get this out of the way.' Sloane closes her laptop and slips it into the bag at her feet. 'Bad habit.'

'It's fine,' I say. 'I'm the same.' Then I add, '*Was* the same.'

'So,' she says. 'Realistically, how are things looking with the retrial?'

I draw a breath. 'Challenging,' I say. 'Challenging, but we are making progress. His lawyer, Lawrence Roth, gives it a fifty per cent chance.'

'One thing a podcast can do is bring people forward, anyone who has information they didn't think was relevant, or something might click and someone realises their husband or brother was out that night. I don't know. I'm hoping we can help, not just investigate but raise awareness too.'

'Sure,' I say. 'I mean, we have had press, it's one of the most famous cases in this country's history.'

'Sorry, I didn't mean—'

'No, no, it's fine. I know what you're saying. New audiences, more ears, more people thinking about it.'

She exhales, reaches for her wine. 'I really don't want to step on toes. I just want to know where we are at. What's happening with the court and the appeals.'

'Well, we are getting traction. We're mounting another appeal next month, but it's a slow-moving beast.'

'And how is he doing?'

'He's fine. It's been almost two decades, so he's used to life inside. After a while I guess the mind grows accustomed to the violence and isolation of prison. The one thing he talks about a lot is the idea that people believe he is a murderer, and that there might be a killer still out in the world.'

'Sure,' she says.

'The *Herald* ran a poll last year: eighty-five per cent guilty, nine per cent innocent, six per cent undecided.'

She clamps her mouth closed, a vein at her temple. 'Right.' She drags her fingers back through her hair. 'And a newspaper conducted the poll? They didn't think there was anything unethical about that?'

'They pulled it down. It was online.'

'Those polls – whenever anyone does them, they're not real. They're not a fair or accurate reflection of the populace. I've seen behind the curtain. They are *always* hijacked. Groups spam them with fake votes. So just ignore that. I think if we get a retrial, you'll see it's not right.'

There's something about the way she says *we*. The ownership. It does suggest she's on our side, but also that she's got some part to play, like this is *her* case.

'Bill has asked for my advice, as you know. He wants me to make sure you're on the right side.' After my last visit, I think he's more likely to speak with Sloane than me right now.

'The right side?'

'I don't know that he's innocent, but I know he didn't get a fair trial. He's never acknowledged any guilt or culpability. If he's guilty, he's the best liar I've ever met. He only wants to speak to you for the podcast if you come into this with the assumption of innocence.'

Her expression is neutral. 'Well, I'm open-minded, like my audience, but I don't have all the facts and that's why I'm here.

I can't come in with the assumption of innocence, I can't come into it with any assumptions at all.'

I keep her fixed in my gaze. She's easy enough to read – maintaining eye contact, a relaxed posture, pinching the stem of her wine glass.

'I want to hear anything you plan to share. I want it first.'

'No copy approval, I said—'

'No, no, I just want to hear it first. Not change it, just prepare for it. And anything you find that might help the case, you share with us. Me and his lawyer.'

'Of course. No questions asked.'

'We're getting close, Sloane. But I have to tell you this is his life, and I've put my heart and soul into getting him out, so if this is just about ratings, and advertising revenue—'

She lets out a small laugh and squeezes the bridge of her nose. '*Please*, we were getting on so well. Don't insult me.'

'I didn't mean—'

'Okay, now you listen to me,' she begins, her voice even and assured. 'I hopped on a flight. I listened to your demands. I'm grateful you've decided to bring me in, but if you think I do this for anything, *anything*, other than justice, then I'll just get back on that plane and go home. I've made a career out of getting the truth. If Bill is innocent, *really* innocent, then you have nothing to worry about.'

'I hear you loud and clear.'

A presence over my shoulder.

'Give us a minute, we've not had a chance to look at the menu just yet,' Sloane says, barely breaking eye contact with me. She waits a moment before speaking again, now a little lower. 'Here's the thing about it, TK. I think you might be too close, too invested. I think you're afraid I'll press at the sore spots, the weaknesses in his defence, and I might find something you don't want to know about. I want to record a podcast about this case, warts and all, so that's exactly what I'm going to do. You can get me the access to Bill, or you can keep him from me. But one thing I will not do is produce an eight-to-ten-episode puff piece.'

I swallow hard. I can't keep her from him, and I probably can't influence Bill at all until I visit again and apologise – will he give me a chance to explain?

She speaks so clearly, so directly, in a way I'm not used to. It might just be one of those fine distinctions between Aussies and Kiwis – we inherited the British reticence, the resistance to direct conflict – it's clear Sloane did not. She's tackling the elephant in the room and bringing it down hard. I almost admire it.

'Well,' I say. 'I want the truth as much as anyone. But I also want Bill to have a fair go. I don't want the public baying for his blood if we do get this retrial.'

'Sure,' Sloane says. That sweet smile is back. She signals to the waiter and he comes back over. 'You should know that about me by now. I'm not about to feed him to the wolves, TK. Let's start with this manuscript he's written. Can I at least get a copy of that, to see what happened in his words?'

I've read it a number of times; I know there are things in there that Bill hasn't remembered with a great deal of exactitude, but I also know he wants her to have it.

'Okay,' I say. 'That could be a good place to start.'

Course after course of seafood comes out of the kitchen. Oysters, crudo, scallops, a snapper fillet. All small dishes that we share. We chat about life in general, what got Sloane into journalism. We talk about her previous cases in Australia. The small details she thought *had* to be in her previous podcast to honour the victim: a hair clip found in the mud, the victim's nickname at school, Bambi.

'We humanise the victims. Crime stories are about the victim and the victim only. *Never* the perpetrator. We don't give them that.'

*Is Bill one of the victims in this case?* I wonder. But I don't ask. I pushed things before, she put me in my place and the conversation is much easier now.

'Oh, by the way,' she says. 'Have you been into the house? I'm heading down there tomorrow.'

'Don't bother, the new owners won't let you in.'

She smiles. 'Well, I emailed the agent who sold the house, he put me in touch with the owners and they've agreed to give me a tour.'

She notices my mouth hanging open.

'Like I said, TK, I plan on getting to the bottom of this. One way or another.'

I drive her to the hotel, then head home. I sit on the couch in the dark, thinking through everything. I should visit Bill again, explain that Sloane is going ahead whether or not we are onboard.

# EIGHT
## SLOANE

I'VE LOST COUNT of the times people have thrust a manuscript at me, asking for help to get it published. At my best friend's wedding, her mother-in-law bailed me up at the bar for half an hour, telling me about her father's biography she wants to write; my personal trainer got me at my most vulnerable in the depths of a hellish bum-and-tum workout with a pitch for his crime novel; Rain's cousin emailed me directly with his idea for a sci-fi novel . . . the list goes on. It's as if they think I have the keys to some secret club, and I decide who comes and goes. The truth is, I'm just as mystified by the choices publishers make as everyone else, and I have zero sway over what they choose to publish. Having a couple of modestly successful true crime books under my belt doesn't help. But, despite my aversion to unsolicited manuscripts, reading Bill's memoir is actually refreshing. One: it wasn't thrust onto me; two: it's not poorly written – it could do with a little work, and a lot of refining, but the story is *compelling*. I got through the first three chapters last night before turning in, and now as I drive my rental from Auckland down to Cambridge to visit the murder house, I can't stop thinking about it.

I haven't booked accommodation, but I figure I'll stay somewhere local, get a feel for the place and see if I can track down anyone who knew the Primrose family. Maybe visit the local schools – someone there may remember the kids.

Despite supposedly being on leave, Tara has been busy sending out mass emails, trying to track down anyone who worked at the house or was involved in the case. But we need to be focused and prioritise people who were in or around the house at the time of the murders. She's tracked down the old cleaner and is trying to find a gardener who worked there after Bill's Uncle Mooks was fired.

I drive the rental, a new Rav 4, out of Auckland and down to Cambridge. On the way I listen to a podcast; the host insists it's the number one *underground* true crime podcast, despite the tens of thousands of ratings on the app store – a sure-fire indicator that the podcast is well and truly above sea level now. They have dedicated an episode to the Primrose stabbings. They barely scratch the surface; all the information they cover is publicly available, with no interviews or insights from anyone involved in the case.

I note as I drive the absence of native bush outside. The remorseless industry of colonisers swept through in the nineteenth century, I suppose. Where there once might have been ferns, scrub, trees, there are only endless green paddocks, alternately speckled with birch-coloured sheep and black-and-white cows. And in the distance, those conical mountain peaks that slowly slide past on the horizon until they're in the rear-view mirror.

The smaller towns seem to have Māori names, while the cities and larger towns still wear titles the colonisers carried across the sea. Cambridge, I find, is quaint with just a couple of small cafes, shops and a service station. An opportunity shop. The usual fare. In a blink the town is behind me and I'm travelling along another rural road into the country. Big farmhouses are set back from the road. Fenced in paddocks of horses, cows, sheep. Less than a minute later, I turn down a rambling road, a horse truck passing me the other way. It's not far now. I've travelled just a minute or two from town before I'm pulling in at a gate.

'Hello?' a woman's voice answers when I buzz.

'Hi, my name's Sloane. We've been emailing.'

'Oh, hi, yes, I'll buzz you through. Terry is here too, waiting.'

The house is set about thirty metres back from the road, at the end of a serpentine, paved driveway, overhung by trees on one side and opening up to gardens on the other. It's not particularly well kept, but then the owners haven't been living here too long. The house itself is grand, if a little dated, two storeys tall with a stone façade. Nothing like any of the other houses I passed along the way here. It is a beautiful building, despite what happened here.

I park near the entrance, beneath a covered carport. A golden retriever comes bounding toward my car, tail wagging, as a woman steps through the front door. She's late fifties, blonde hair, smiling eyes. She calls the dog over as I open my door and step out.

'Hi,' she says, coming forward and offering her hand. 'Marie.'

'Sloane,' I say, matching her smile.

'It's so nice to meet you, I listened to your podcast.'

'Oh, I'm glad to hear.'

'Come,' she says, turning to let me through the door. 'This way.'

The house feels somehow larger than it looked in the crime scene photos that I'd seen. Marie takes me past the base of the stairs, through the living area to the dining area.

A man looks up at me over his reading glasses, assessing me for a moment before he stands. 'Terrence De Koening.'

'Sloane,' I say. His grip is just a little too strong, and he has a natural air of authority about him.

'Please, take a seat.'

He shuffles the pages on the table before him, stacking them to one side. Marie and Terrence sit down.

'So,' I begin, removing the voice recorder from my bag, 'I'll try not to keep you long. I just had a few questions about the house.'

As I place the recorder on the table, Terrence's hand reaches out, covering it. He shakes his head. 'We don't want to be part of your podcast,' he says.

'Sorry?'

'I said, we don't want to be part of your podcast, please don't record our voices.'

I blink away the confusion. 'Okay, sorry, I was under the impression from your emails—'

'Yes, you've had your assistant harass us for this conversation—'

'Terrence,' Marie says. 'She's a guest—'

'Sorry, there must be some confusion. Harass?' My head swims. 'As far as I'm concerned there's been no harassment, our correspondence has been entirely cordial.' He doesn't speak, he simply levels me with his gaze. 'Let's put that aside. If you're not happy for me to record, that's fine. I can just ask you a few questions about the house.'

'So you're going to try get him out?' Terrence says. It seems like a non sequitur; he clearly has a chip on his shoulder.

'I'm not trying to do anything other than get to the heart of the story. I want to give my listeners an opportunity to make their minds up themselves.'

A hack of laughter. 'Right, well if your listeners had half a brain they'd trust the robust legal process.'

'We've had tourists try to visit the house. People think it's odd that we live here,' Marie says.

'They don't realise how much work we've done. It's not the same house. We completely gutted the inside. All of this is new,' Terrence says, gesturing expansively. 'We knocked over the cottage where Bill Ruatara lived. It was too good a deal to pass up, especially with property prices being the way they are.'

'That's right,' Marie adds.

I realise they want to use this interview as a mechanism for defending themselves. They probably copped a bit of flak from locals for moving in here. But Terrence makes a valid point. It sounds like it sold for roughly half its value. 'We're just concerned your podcast is going to bring a whole lot of attention to something that is done and dusted.'

'Right,' I say. 'Well, I'm here to record this podcast.'

Terrence's nostrils flare. 'There are so many unsolved crimes. Why are you bothering with one that is solved?'

I realise I need to quickly get them onside here. I give a warm smile, pull my voice recorder from where it is still wedged under Terrence's palm and put it away in my bag. I take out my notepad instead.

'Look, I hear what you are saying. The last thing I want to do is make life difficult for you both. The podcast is happening, and as there is a continued push for Bill Ruatara's release, there will be growing interest in your house. That's just a fact. What you can do is be proactive. You've said the house has changed a lot, right? And your reasoning for buying it, given the climate of the property market, is sound. Tabloids will dredge up the past, they'll speculate on the purchase and release details. If we talk about it first, if I include those details in the podcast, then fans, er, listeners will sympathise with you and understand your need for privacy.'

He's watching me closely, I glance at Marie. She seems more receptive.

'Terry retired two years ago,' Marie says, turning to her husband. As she talks, sharp lines appear in her make-up. 'We only have our nest egg now. That's we why we sold up and moved here.'

'Again, it's a totally valid reason,' I say, looking around me. 'The house is objectively beautiful.'

'Terry?' she says. He sniffs.

'It's not just the house,' he says.

'Yeah?'

He clears his throat. 'I was headmaster at St Luke's from 2001 until 2015.'

'You knew the family?'

He nods. 'Not well. But yeah, I knew them. Half the town knew them. I don't want their lives to be some show, entertainment for ghouls around the world. They deserve that.'

I nod again. 'Have you listened to my previous podcast, Terrence?'

'No, not yet. But she liked it.' He jerks his head at his wife. 'I don't much listen to podcasts. I mostly just read books, play piano.'

'Well, I like to think I give the victims the centre stage. I like to think I am kind and treat them with the dignity and respect they deserve. Not salacious, no airing of dirty laundry, unless it is directly pertinent to the case.'

I notice in my periphery that Marie is nodding. It's clear she's leading the charge here, that she organised this, probably against his better judgement.

'Well,' he says at last, rising. 'I suppose I should make us a cup of tea and we can have that talk.'

•

Terrence tells me everything about the purchase of the house, how he and Marie had always admired it, the fact that it was much cheaper than it ought to have been because of its history. Elizabeth Primrose was the executor of the family trust; it was sold on to developers who failed to get any traction with a redevelopment, then Terrence and Marie put an offer in. The interior was graffitied beyond recognition. Every window smashed, candles burnt presumably from some seance by kids on a dare. The pool was littered with road cones, a shopping trolley, drug paraphernalia. The roof was leaking. They put hundreds of thousands of dollars into restoring the property and, Terrence adds proudly, it's come out wonderfully.

'And you mentioned you knew the family?'

'Only in a professional setting,' Terrance said. 'A late enrolment from memory, and the girl had some issues at school. A regrettable, close friendship with a physical education teacher.'

I make a note on my pad about this – this is the first I've heard of trouble at school.

'Could I ask you to give me a tour?' I say casually, after we've been speaking for almost an hour.

'Come on then,' Terrence says, as Marie begins to clear the table.

He takes me through the downstairs rooms, pointing out which ones have changed and how. Then he takes me upstairs. I feel a cool tickle at my throat. *This is where it happened*, I remind myself. My eyes search for spots of blood I know aren't there. The stairs wrap the foyer, leading to a landing, where a hallway runs one way to the kids' bedrooms, and the other way to the master bedroom and guest room.

The first bedroom we stop at is on the north side of the house, the afternoon sun is filling the room. It's got a desk in one corner and art on the walls. There's a stationary bike set up facing the window, with views over the back yard.

'This one was the daughter's,' Terrence says. *How well did he know her?* 'Now it's my study and gym.' I can't help but glance at him. He's very tall and in reasonable shape, I suppose, for a man of his age. But he doesn't strike me as a fitness junkie. He turns back and I see veins in his pink ruddy cheeks. Despite the warmth in the room, a cool breeze runs over my skin. I imagine a young girl, on the floor before me, blood pulsing from a gaping wound in her stomach.

Terrence leaves the room and I follow him out.

'The son was in here,' he says at the next room. He doesn't use their names.

'Did you know him? He was at middle school, wasn't he?'

'That's right. I never met him, but he seemed to be a good kid.'

This room is now a library by the looks of it. Shelves of books, a reading chair, a sewing machine set up on a table and views out over the front lawn toward the road. It's much cooler, I notice, than the last bedroom.

'Marie reads her books, does her sewing up here. She doesn't like it. Thinks the room has bad energy.'

I could laugh at the irony.

Then he takes me to the master bedroom.

'This is our room, it's all different now. The shape's the same but we replaced the carpet in the bedrooms, it was torn up and waterlogged. We made the walk-in wardrobe bigger, cutting into the bathroom. We pulled the bath out of the en suite and renovated it all. I understand the bed used to be over here.' He gestures to the far wall. 'Coming out this way. We decided it was better under the window on this wall because you get a bit of morning sun in summer.' He turns back, smiles for the first time. 'Not a bad view of the front garden, eh?'

'It's nice,' I lie.

'We replaced the old curtains. Even if they weren't torn and moth-eaten, we would have gotten rid of them. They were an old paisley, really not our style.'

'Can I ask, did you notice anything off when you started renovating?'

'Such as?'

'Well, um, anything that might have belonged to the family? Or anything that struck you as not quite right?'

'Well . . . I wasn't sure if I should mention this or not,' he says, rolling up each sleeve of his shirt. 'Come on, I think you'll be very interested in something in the basement.'

He leads me downstairs, through the living room and then the dining room, where Marie is wiping down the table, and opens the door to the basement.

'I told one of the local cops about it. He didn't seem to think it was important, but it might be good for your podcast. I reckon, if anything, it proves Ruatara did it even more.'

He hits the lights and I can see all the way into the cavernous space under the house.

'Two things,' he says. 'One: it's not that common to see a basement like this in New Zealand. It's a bit of a flood risk, actually. As you can see, we don't keep much down here. When we moved in, we found a couple of things that probably belonged to the Primrose family. An old set of golf clubs,' he says pointing toward the corner. 'They're still there. Must have been Simon's. And the second thing is this.'

He nods at a gas heating unit on the wall. Beside it is a six-foot-tall gas bottle.

'Definitely not common in New Zealand, especially back then. We are a cold country, but everyone uses fires to heat their homes, or electric heating. Gas central heating isn't a big thing out here in the country, especially fifteen years ago before the greenies started moaning about burning wood.'

'I suppose that's odd.'

He turns to me, and the way the naked bulb shadows his eyes makes my heart speed up.

'No, that's not the odd thing. We use it, it's great actually. It's ducted to all the rooms, so it heats the entire place like a dream. After all this time we had to have someone come out and give it a service, to check it still works fine.'

Footsteps on the stairs. I turn and see Marie standing at the top, looking down. I have an odd sense of claustrophobia. *I need to get out*, I think. What is it about this place, these people, that makes me so scared?

'So that's what you thought I'd be interested in?' I say.

'Not the fact they had central heating like this, no. It was what the heating guy found. The exhaust of the heater was clogged with leaves, twigs, debris.'

'So after all the years it got blocked?'

'Well, he said it was practically impossible for that to happen naturally. If you see where it comes out, you'll realise the filters prevent anything from coming back down it. And it was all in one spot, as if someone jammed it in there. Even if it built up naturally over the years, the other thing was this valve,' he says, pointing at the heater. 'It opens when carbon monoxide backs up into the body of the unit, and that was definitely tampered with. He said that was sealed shut with silicon.'

I'm trying to understand what this means when he volunteers the information.

'If the exhaust is blocked and the safety valve fails, carbon monoxide ends up pumping through the system,' he says, running his hand over his head. 'I reckon he tried to kill them this way, then when that didn't work, he stabbed them.'

'Why didn't it work?'

'Probably too big, too many ways for the carbon monoxide to escape. Anyway, like I said, the local coppers didn't think it was worth bothering with.'

'Have you got any photos?'

'Marie has a couple on her phone.'

I walk further into the basement, my heart hammering. It's much more spacious than it looks; the further you go in, the more it reveals itself. I move through the gloom toward the corner. Wooden pillars stand, evenly spaced, like tall, pale men watching me pass. Apparently no-one else has lived here since the Primrose family, and almost everything was cleared out. Who knows where it all ended up, but there's a box covered in dust, it appears recently opened. When I go closer, I see there are a few old books. *Encyclopaedia Britannica* scrawled on the spine of each. Not a full set, just two or three.

I see the golf clubs. An old dusty set.

'Can I touch them?' I say. I can see finger marks in the dust. It's clear Terrence or someone else has handled them recently.

'Be my guest.'

I pull one out, hold it in my hands, study it for a moment.

'Lefty,' Terrence says.

*Lefty.* I take my notebook out and make a note.

'Mind if I take a photo?' I say.

'Be my guest.'

I snap a couple of images of the putter.

It's with relief that I emerge back into the main house. Marie shows me the photos of the blocked exhaust, I see all the dry foliage, it looks like it had been there for a long time. I feel warmth in my chest, a tingling inside. I realise this is something, this is exactly why I do this. Before I leave, I note one or two further details about the house. In a bookcase in the living room, there are a number of books on flyfishing and New Zealand history. But then shelved beside them are two true crime books. Both about what happened in this house. *The Primrose Stabbings. Cold Hands.*

Terrence notices me looking.

'I've read them both, a number of times before we bought the house. I'm just as certain as anybody that he did it.'

He reaches out and takes *The Primrose Stabbings* from the shelf. 'This one was written by one of the arresting officers. I suggest you read it, if you haven't already. Ruatara's a monster, and he did what monsters do.'

'Thanks. I'll add it to the reading pile.'

In the car on the way to the motel I message TK. *Call me ASAP.*

'Sloane,' he says, calling me immediately.

'Do you know anything about a blocked gas heater exhaust at the house?'

'What?'

'Yeah, I just visited. The new owners found that the gas heater was deliberately tampered with; it was likely pumping carbon monoxide into the house.'

'Holy shit,' he says. 'Sorry, darling. Holy ship, I mean. I've got my daughter.'

*Daughter.* I had no idea.

'This is big, Sloane. Did you get any photos?'

'A couple,' I say. 'But listen, I'll try to speak with the guy who repaired it, the owners gave me his contact number. They didn't want to be part of the podcast. He was the old headmaster at St Luke's. Terrence De Koening.'

'I knew I'd heard that name before. And he thought he'd just live in the house where one of his students and her family were stabbed?'

'He's funny. Seems to like the building. They got it for a song, and the renovation is nice. I got a slightly creepy vibe just being in that house, though. I couldn't live there.'

'No. I've got good news for you too,' he says. 'Bill is happy to see you.'

I smile, following the GPS to the motel. 'Brilliant. Thank you. When?'

'I'll organise it, but I need to do that before I go.'

'Tomorrow?' I eye the rear-view mirror; it feels like the car behind me has been following me for a while. I block it out, still feeling uncomfortable after being in that house.

'Tomorrow works. In the afternoon.'

'I'll let you know.'

I stop at a pizza place in town. The diet and exercise regime I was planning is already out the window. I pick up a small Hawaiian and a bottle of Merlot.

•

Apparently someone thought it was a good idea to schedule a national cycling race beginning and ending in town this weekend. Apparently the only available accommodation in Cambridge is the Pacific Inn Motor Lodge, with a jaw-dropping one star and a rating of 2.9 on TripAdvisor. When I arrive, I realise why it's the last place booked out. I should have opted for an Airbnb out of town, but I guess this will have to do.

Waikeria Prison, where Bill is housed, is about forty minutes away.

The motel receptionist is spritely, all things considered. It's clear she lives above the reception. When I press the button on the door, a few minutes later she comes bounding down the stairs to check me in.

She hands over the keys and says, 'There's nowhere to park outside your room. I suggest parking over there outside unit eleven. I can help with your bags.'

'It's fine,' I say. 'Thanks.'

'One night, right?' she says.

'Yep,' I say. I don't ask about extending my stay because I'm hoping to find somewhere else online tonight. I open the boot, unzip my suitcase and find my toiletries, pyjamas, clean undies and a clean t-shirt, laptop and recording equipment. I shove it all in my tote bag; the rest can stay in the boot overnight. I heave it all across the expanse of the car park to my room.

I call Tara and bring her up to speed.

'No way,' she says. 'Blocked with what?'

'Foliage from the garden, mostly, by the sounds of it. Just leaves and sticks shoved down there. Apparently it couldn't have gotten in there unless someone did it deliberately.'

'Well I think we have the hook for the first episode.'

'I'll chat with Esteban,' I say. My producer may want to take it a different direction, but I agree it's a strong opening. Especially given the fact it's a scoop – there's nothing about it at all online, or in the media.

I should start recording, but instead I pull Bill's manuscript out and continue reading, this new context and my own experience in the house having added texture to an already gripping story. But soon enough I'm dozing off. I brush my teeth; the hot and cold taps are reversed and the toilet paper holder is hanging on by a single screw. I think of the five-star hotel I stayed in after the media awards in Sydney. It's all part of the story, I suppose, tomorrow the pillow will be plump and sheets crisp.

My sleep has been better in the months since I abandoned my personal social media accounts. I've not been sleeping with my phone in the bedroom, but now I keep it close to hand. A big girl like me, rattled by a slightly creepy ex-headmaster? Couldn't be.

But I do feel something, a tension under my sternum, a tightness in my throat. I think about the stalker, could they have followed me over here? There's really no evidence of it. That's half the reason I jumped on the first flight, and how would they know where I am?

My room is too close to the road, and every time a truck passes, the place seems to rattle. Sometime around 2 am, I wake. I was dreaming, I don't know about what, but I thought I heard breaking glass. False alarm. I sit up and open my laptop. I find myself searching the case again. I'm obsessed. This is what it takes. Even at this time of night I hear a car pass out on the road. The rest of the night I toss and turn. I can't identify the exact feeling: trepidation, excitement, fear, a mixture of all? I think I had this with the last podcast, when I realised we could make a difference, when I realised we were exploring the negative space between police evidence and our own findings, the coincidences were lining up, and there was heat and movement. Now it's happening again. Whether or not Bill Ruatara is guilty, there are clearly elements of this case that have been overlooked.

When I wake in the morning, I leave a message with Andrew from Cambridge Gas and Plumbing. He's happy to be recorded for the podcast. Then I pack up and head out to the car. That's the problem. The car. Where I parked it last night, I find nothing but a splash of glass shards in the gravel.

'Fuck,' I say, quietly at first. Then a little louder. 'Fuck, fuck, fuck.'

**hachette**
AUSTRALIA

If you would like to find out more about Hachette Australia, our authors, upcoming events and new releases, you can visit our website or our social media channels:

hachette.com.au

 HachetteAustralia

HachetteAus